WHERE WAS THE HURON?

Vallian crouched suddenly, squatting at the foot of the tree, then he moved suddenly, swiftly, crouched low. He felt a cold chill of panic run through him.

The Huron!

He was out there . . . he had to be stalking *him!* Vallian had heard stories about the man. He was a skillful hunter and he had killed more than one man. He was like a ghost in the woods, and in this timber along the river he was in his element.

Vallian strained his ears for sound, heard nothing. He was good, he told himself, but was he as good as the Huron? Was he even half as good?

Bantam Books by Louis L'Amour
Ask your bookseller for the books you have missed

THE QUICK AND THE DEAD
LOUIS L'AMOUR

BANTAM BOOKS
TORONTO · NEW YORK · LONDON · SYDNEY

THE QUICK AND THE DEAD

A Bantam Book | November 1973
12 printings through May 1979
Revised Bantam edition | July 1979
2nd printing .... April 1980
3rd printing .... June 1980
4th printing .... May 1981

Photograph of Louis L'Amour
by John Hamilton—Globe Photos, Inc.

ISBN 0–553–20180–8

Published simultaneously in the United States and Canada

PRINTED IN THE UNITED STATES OF AMERICA

13 12 11 10 9 8 7

Chapter I

When Susanna stepped down from the wagon Duncan had the fire going, but he sat staring into the flames, forearms resting on his knees, hands hanging loose.

"Duncan?" She was a slender, graceful and unusually pretty woman. "Duncan? What is it?"

"It's this . . . all of it." His gesture took in their surroundings. "I had no right to bring you and Tom into this, no right at all."

"We discussed it, Duncan. We all took part in the decision. We all decided it was the best thing."

"I know, Susanna, but that was back east. It was one thing to sit in a comfortable living room and talk about the west, but it's something else when you are face to face with it." He looked westward, toward the open plains. "What's out there, Susanna? What are we getting into?"

"Somebody's coming, Pa." Tom was twelve. If his father had doubts, he had none.

They looked where he pointed. A rider was coming

1

through the scattered trees toward them. He was a tall, rough-looking man on a roan horse, and he carried his rifle as if born with it.

He pulled up some fifty yards off. His eyes swept the camp "Howdy. All right if I come in?"

There was nothing about his looks to inspire confidence but Duncan McKaskel said, "Come on in. It's all right."

He rode up, stopping across the fire from their wagon, dismounting with his horse between himself and the fire.

"Seen your smoke. Figured you might have coffee."

Rifle in hand he walked to the fire, seeing Susanna he removed his hat. "Sorry, ma'am. Don't like to butt in like this but I been ridin' all night, an' no coffee for three, four days."

"Be seated. Breakfast will soon be ready."

"I am Duncan McKaskel. My wife Susanna, my son, Tom."

"Howdy."

He added a stick to the fire, glancing at the wagon and the deep-cut tracks. "You got quite a load there. Ain't goin' far, I guess."

"We're going west," Duncan said.

"You ain't goin' far with that load." He accepted the cup Susanna poured for him and squatted on his heels. "You got four head of mules out there . . . good mules. But that's too much load."

"We will manage," Duncan's tone was cool.

The stranger was, Susanna decided, very good-looking in a rough way. He wore a mustache, was unshaved, and his boots were down at the heel. All his clothes were shabby, yet there was an animal strength about him and an almost feline grace.

"Good coffee." He reached for the pot and refilled his cup. "Ever driven on the prairie? I mean where there's no road?"

"No, I háven't."

"Had a sign of rain lately. The grass is good for the stock, but it makes the pullin' mighty hard. You ain't goin' far with just four mules an' a load that heavy. An' s'posin' your mules wander off? How'll you find 'em?"

"We have riding horses."

The stranger sipped his coffee. "Not no more, you don't. They've been took."

"What's that?"

"You had you a pair of sorrels? Big, handsome horses?"

"Yes."

"Then you don't have them no longer. They been stole."

"What's that?" McKaskel came to his feet. "What do you mean?"

"A couple of fellers drove them off just before full light. Fellers from the settlement, yonder."

"I don't believe—" McKaskel started to move off, then glanced from the stranger to Susanna. He stopped. "Tom, you run and check on the horses."

Susanna was slicing bacon into the frying-pan, her face flushed from the heat. "You're a mighty handsome woman, ma'am."

"Thank you."

"When you crossed the river, yonder? You come right up through the settlement?"

"We stopped there." McKaskel decided he did not like this man.

"Figured you had. They seen your stock, and they seen your woman."

"What do you mean by that?"

"That's a mean outfit. Small caliber, but mean. They seen that heavy-loaded wagon, your wife, an' your stock. They mean to have them."

Tom came running, his face white. "Pa! The horses are gone! There's tracks . . . right across that sandy place toward those shacks."

McKaskel felt sick. He had known there might be trouble in coming west, but felt sure that if he minded his own business he could stay out of it. He got up slowly, then went to the wagon for his rifle.

"Duncan . . . ?" Susanna was frightened.

"I must have those horses. I'll just walk over and see if I can find them."

The stranger picked two slices of bacon from the skillet. Without looking up he said, "You ever kill a man, McKaskel?"

"Kill a man?" McKaskel was startled. "Why, no. I haven't."

"You walk into that settlement with that gun an' you better figure on it."

"I don't think—"

"Mister, folks say this country is hell on horses an' women. Well, it's hell on tenderfeet, too. You walk into that place without bein' ready to kill an' your wife'll be a widow before the hour's gone."

"That's nonsense. I'll go to the law."

"Ain't none. Folks out here generally make their own."

"I can use this rifle. I've killed a dozen deer—"

"Was the deer shootin' back at you? Mister, that outfit figure on you comin' in. They want you to. Why do you s'pose they left all them tracks? They figure to kill you, Mister."

"What?"

"They seen your woman. That gang figures your stock and your wagonload are worth somethin'. They took your horses so you'll come lookin'. They want you to come armed. Nobody will ever ask questions, but if they do they'll just say you came in there a-frettin' and a-steamin' and made a fight, so they just had to kill you."

"So what am I to do? Let them steal my horses?"

"Uh-uh. You just go in there with your eyes open, figurin' you're goin' to have to kill somebody. You spot you a big fat man, an' when you start talkin' you just sort of careless-like get your rifle pointed at him. Then you tell them to trot out your horses."

"Duncan? Don't do it. It isn't worth it. Not for two horses."

"We raised those horses, Susanna, and they belong to us. I shall go after them."

"He's got to try, ma'am. If he don't go in they'll foller after an' steal your mules."

"How do you know so much about it?" Susanna demanded. "How do we know you are not one of them?"

His grin was sly, amused. "You don't, ma'am."

"I'm going in," McKaskel said, again.

"You better . . . while the notion's on you. You just go right on in, an' don't you worry none about your woman, here. Anything happens to you an' I'll take care of her. I'll do just that."

"Now, see here!"

"You got it to do, McKaskel. You better have at it."

McKaskel hesitated, glancing from one to the other.

"Duncan," Susanna said quietly, "if it must be done, do it, and do not worry about me. I will be all right."

"Pa? Can I go with you? I can shoot!"

"You stay with your mother."

He took up his rifle and strode out of camp. His mouth was dry and he was frightened. Only three hundred yards to the shacks, and he did not know whether he wished it were nearer or farther. He had seen the men sitting on the saloon porch as he and his family came through and he had been glad to leave them behind.

He thought of his rifle. It was a good one, and he could shoot straight, but he had never shot at a man. Could he do it now? And that stranger back there? He had left his wife and son with him, and how did he know that the stranger was not worse than any of those in the settlement?

The shacks were there, right in front of him. The horses were there, too, tied right to the rail in front of the saloon. No attempt had been made to conceal them. They were a challenge, an affront.

He remembered how they had looked at Susanna. He had planned to drive right out on the prairie, but he had hesitated, for once they left the river and its rim of trees they had left all behind, they were committed to something he now began to see as sheer folly.

Back east, with the west far, far away, it had been a topic of conversation, but the talk had continued until they actually packed up and moved west.

Those men were waiting. He could see two men seated on a rough bench, another standing in the door, and they had seen him coming. He could not turn back now. They would know he was afraid.

The stranger was right. They planned to kill him.

How? It was all so obvious. The horses were there, he had only to walk in, state his ownership and bring them away.

That was all . . . or was it?

Back at the fire the stranger emptied his cup. Susanna's features were white and strained. "Well," the stranger said, "you better make your plans. He went in an' I wouldn't give a busted trace-chain for his chances. You're goin' to be a widow, ma'am. Now I ain't much, but—"

"You're going to let him be killed?"

"None of my affair."

"Help him."

"You his woman?"

"We are married."

"Wasn't what I asked. I wanted to know if you was his woman? It ain't always the same thing."

"I am his woman and am proud to be so. He is a fine man. And I am a decent woman."

Lazily, he got to his feet and moved to his horse. "I'll just mosey on in an' see the fun." He swung into the saddle. "Of course, if he gets himself killed, you got you a choice . . . me or them."

"I shall go back home." Susanna replied. "I am sure Tom and I could get along."

He grinned at her and swung his horse. As soon as

he emerged from the trees he could see McKaskel walking into the street. The stranger turned his horse to use the cover of the trees and came up to the town at an angle from which he could not be seen as he watched McKaskel. Drawing up in the shade of the trees, he drew his rifle from its scabbard.

There really was not much he could do. So much would depend on how the game was played.

He could hear McKaskel speaking. "I see you found my horses. Thank you for holding them for me."

The thin man who answered him seemed amused. "Your horses, you say? Now how would we know that? Those horses come driftin' in, an' my boys tied them up. We figure to keep them."

"They belong to me. I have their papers."

The man grinned lazily, a taunting grin. "Papers? Now, ain't that too bad? I cain't read, Mister. I just cain't make out them words . . . neither can my boy."

McKaskel remembered what the stranger had said. The fat man was lounging in the doorway. McKaskel shifted his feet slightly, and managed to turn the muzzle of his gun, an easy, natural movement, but suddenly it was there, covering the fat man.

"I shall take my horses. I am sure you will thank your son for me, but tell them we reared these horses and we must keep them. We intend to keep them."

He stepped toward the horses.

The thin man spat lazily. "Mister, was you to untie them horses somebody might get the idea you was tryin' to steal them. You ready to get yourself shot?"

McKaskel kept his eyes on the fat man as he spoke to the thin one. "Even if I was to get shot I'd still pull this trigger, and I couldn't miss that man standing in the door."

The rifle tilted ever so little, and he kept the fat man covered as he pulled the string to untie the knot.

"Don't nobody do nothin' foolish!" The fat man shouted the words. "Let 'im go!"

Holding the rifle ready, Duncan McKaskel put a

foot in the stirrup and swung to the saddle. Turning his horse he untied the second horse, keeping his rifle in position as he did so.

He backed the horses into the street, keeping the rifle on the fat man, but as he turned the horses his rifle swung off target and on the instant the fat man disappeared into the saloon and the men on the porch threw themselves right and left, one of them scrambling toward the open door.

There were two shots.

Duncan McKaskel heard them both, and in an instant of stark panic he realized he had been perfectly set up, the horses and the men on the porch drawing his full attention while the real danger lay behind him.

He felt the *whiff* of the bullet past his cheek at the instant he heard the ugly bark of two shots, the sound of one shot almost lost in the sound of the other.

Turning his horse sharply to face the street, his rifle up, he found the street empty. The men were gone from the porch, but from the loft door of the barn opposite the saloon hung the body of a man, his head and one arm visible.

In the dappled shadow of the trees near the entrance to the street was the stranger, holding a rifle in his hand.

"Just back off easy now, and if anything moves, shoot."

Rifle on the street, McKaskel rode diagonally away from town, keeping his rifle on target. Turning sharply then, he trotted his horse away under cover of the trees. Suddenly he was shaking all over, and his stomach felt empty and sick.

"I want to get out of here," he said aloud. "I want to get out right now."

The stranger was gone. It had been he who shot the man in the loft door.

Chapter II

Susanna was standing out from the trees, shading her eyes toward the town. When she saw him coming she walked back to the fire. She edged the coffee toward the flames, then turned toward Tom.

"Better bring up the mules, Tom. Water them and bring them up."

Reluctantly, the boy turned away. He had seen his father coming and longed to hear what happened.

Duncan McKaskel rode into the clearing leading the other sorrel. "We must go now."

"Tom's gone for the mules. You had better eat something."

"No . . . just coffee."

He accepted the cup, took a swallow, then looked at her, his face gray with shock. "Susanna, they were ready for me. I was thinking of the horses and the men on the porch, and there was a man in the loft behind me with a rifle."

"What happened?"

"That man . . . the one who had coffee here. He killed the man in the loft."

"You're alive, Duncan. It's all right."

"A man is dead. He was killed because of me."

"He was killed because he was a thief. When a man takes a gun in his hand against other men he must expect to be killed. He becomes the enemy of all men when he breaks the laws of society."

They were an hour out upon the plains and at least three miles on the road before the subject came up again. "We are not finished with them, Susanna. I believe they will follow us."

"All right." She feigned composure for she did not want him to see her fear. She must show her faith in him. "You know what to expect now."

"Yes . . yes, I do. But I've never killed a man, Susanna, and I don't want to."

"Yet if that man had not been killed, they would have killed you. Tom and I would have been alone."

"Or with that man."

"I'd go home, Duncan. I'd go back and try to get a job teaching school. After all, I have much more education than most women."

"Education." He shook his head. "Susanna, I have always been proud of my education but I am beginning to wonder if we must not begin all over. It is a different time, a different world out here."

The river and the horizon seemed to melt into one. There was no line of demarkation anywhere, only the long grass bending in silver ripples like waves before the wind, and it was empty, like the sky.

The horses were tied behind the wagon and Tom rode at the tail-gate where he could watch them and the trail behind. The mules were in good shape but they seemed to be making harder work of it than they should. Several times he drew up to let them rest, worried at each stop for fear of pursuit. Horsemen could overtake them in no time, and he remembered what that rider had said about his wagon being loaded too heavily.

During one of the stops he walked behind the wagon and was shocked to see how deeply the wheels were cutting into the turf. It *was* a heavy load, and they had far to go.

Susanna's thoughts returned to that man. Ignorant obviously, and a brute . . . yet he had saved her husband's life at some risk to his own and with nothing to gain. She thought of it as a chivalrous act, something she found difficulty in associating with ignorance.

Suppose Duncan had been killed? What would she have done?

The thought frightened her. To return meant to go back through that town . . . no, not that. She would have to drive up river or down and try to find another crossing. But there might be other people like that back there.

She glanced curiously at her husband. He was staring at the empty plains, frowning slightly. Before they left the wagon train because of the outbreak of cholera she had heard stories of what the vast plains did to people. Men had gone insane from that appalling emptiness, unable to cope with such a change.

Duncan had been shaken by what had happened, finding it hard to believe there could not have been some other way, some better way. She knew how he felt, or thought she did.

Duncan was a gentleman, by breeding as well as education. His family was an old Scottish-English family as was her own. In America they had produced clergymen, physicians, teachers, and statesmen as well as planters. Some branches of the family had wealth, unfortunately, theirs did not.

Too proud to live in genteel poverty they had chosen to go west. They had no desire to seek gold, for to them wealth lay in the ownership of land and in its cultivation. They wished to find a green valley where they could sink roots and live out their lives.

Now they were alone, and until now she had not realized what loneliness meant, nor what it had meant to live in an ordered, law-abiding community. There had been occasional thefts, and she could remember a murder once, some years before, but the law had been there, and public opinion, with its protective shield of what was accepted and what was not.

There had been so many restraints, legal and social, between them and the savagery that lay innate in so many people. Out here the bars were down. There was no such restraint . . . not yet.

Duncan drew up again. "Got to rest the mules again. It's hard on them, with no proper trail."

"Do you think that man was right? Are we loaded too heavily?"

Duncan shook his head, but his eyes did not meet hers. "What could we get rid of? Some of those things belonged to your family."

"Yes, yes, I know." The thought stayed with her. Did she really need them? Yet the thought of leaving her things behind gave her a pang. She would need furniture when they made a new home and it would be nice to have them then.

If they ever got there.

"I wonder where he is?" she asked suddenly.

"Who?" he asked, but he knew the answer.

He was thinking that a blind man could follow their deep-cut tracks, and it was now two hours until noon and they had come nine miles. It was good time . . . or would have been had they not been so eager to put distance between them and the river.

His eyes swept the country . . . vast, empty, still. Above them a buzzard soared. How like a speck they must seem to him, a speck in this tremendous ocean of grass. He started the team again but he did not ride the wagon. He walked beside it.

Noon came and passed, but nobody mentioned hunger. Nor was there any place to stop. It was all the same, only the grass, the sky, and the soft wind.

At mid-afternoon they came up to a buffalo wallow. There was water in it, collected from the rains. He unharnessed the team and led them to water, then let them graze for an hour before hitching up again.

The sun was down before they reached Black Jack Creek, and he drove the team through and up the other side, then along the creek for a short distance before stopping.

Duncan found a flat place and started to gather wood. When he put the wood down to start a fire, a voice said, "Don't do that. There's a better place down here."

He turned sharply, realizing he had left his gun in the wagon, and cursing himself for a fool.

The stranger was standing under the edge of the trees, watching him.

"Where'd you come from?" he demanded.

"Been waitin' for you all. I got no coffee, and after that shootin' I didn't figure to ride into town and buy none."

There was a fold in the ground where a trickle of a spring ran down to the creek. On a flat bench beside the spring he had built a small fire. "Can't see it until you're close up," he explained. "No use showin' 'em where you are."

"Do you think they'll come?"

"Uh-huh . . . couple, maybe three hours from now. They'll ride out, scout around, locate your wagon. Maybe they'll run off your stock."

"You don't seem very worried about it."

"Ain't my stock.'

"We haven't thanked you." Susanna had come up behind them. "You saved my husband's life."

"It wasn't nothing. I never liked that Ike Mantle, no way."

She was shocked. "You *knew* him?"

"Oh, sure! He was meaner'n all get-out. His brother Purdy . . . now he's a different kind. He'll shoot you face to face."

He glanced at her. "If'n you're figurin' on eatin', you better get at it. Cook what you got to, then dowse the fire an' set back."

She glanced at him, irritated by his manner.

"Don't take no offense at me, ma'am. I can chew on some jerky an' make out, but that man of yours and the boy, they'll need some cookin', an' you, too, for that matter."

He looked her up and down. "Although you surely do shape up, ma'am. You shape up mighty purty."

"Sir," McKaskel spoke coolly, "you saved my life and you have been very helpful, but I do not like your comments to my wife."

"Well, now." He looked astonished. "You mean you don't think she's got a nice shape? Look at her agin that light. Now—"

"The lady is my wife. I do think her beautiful, but I do not think it is the proper thing to—"

"Think she'll get big headed? Well, maybe so. But she is surely purty. I always did figure it was the right thing to tell either a horse or a woman when they shape up fine. And atop of that she makes good coffee."

Duncan was exasperated, and Susanna had to turn her back so that he could not see her smiling. It was amusing. After all, in his own way he was being complimentary.

When they had eaten, the fire was put out by pulling back the unburned ends of the sticks and thrusting them into the earth to smother the few sparks. The coals that remained would soon die down.

"Take those horses over there behind that fallen tree," he suggested, "an' bed down back yonder. You'll have to keep watch, because sure as shootin', they'll find you."

When Duncan McKaskel led the mules toward the hollow behind the tree, Susanna took the stranger's cup and filled it again. "There's no use throwing the coffee out," she said.

She stopped, holding the pot and looking down at him as he sat on a chunk of wood near the dying fire. "I want to thank you for what you did," she said quietly. "It was a fine thing to do."

He looked at her, then shrugged. "He done all right. I mean he'd have got himself killed because he was all eyes on that porch an' he forgot about what was behind him. In this country you've always got to look behind.

"For a tenderfoot he handled himself mighty well, an' I'd say you got a fair chance." He grinned at her. "Maybe I won't get to pick up the pieces after all."

She filled her own cup. "You might at least tell us your name."

"Names don't count for much out here. Mine's Vallian, Con Vallian. What was your name in the States?"

"Our name in the States?" she was puzzled.

"Sure. Most folks change their names to get away from whoever they are runnin' from."

"Mr. Vallian, we are not *running*. My husband is an honorable man, a man of education, but he wished to be independent of relatives and friends. He wanted to go west where he could make his own way."

"He come to the right place. There ain't no other way out here . . . if he lasts."

He sipped his coffee, then glanced up at Susanna. "You know what they say out here? The educated ones, they find the life and the work too rough and most of them start to drink, and that's the end of them."

"You need not worry, Mr. Vallian. My husband drinks very little, and he is not afraid of hard work."

Con Vallian got to his feet and threw the dregs of his coffee on the coals. "Maybe. We'll have to see how much sand he's got when the going gets rough. Of course," he added, "lots of times it's the womenfolks. Ain't much that's pretty out here, except the country. An' when a man tries farmin' an' gets hailed out, flooded, or froze out, it ain't much fun. If'n he misses those things there's always drouth an' grasshoppers."

"Grasshoppers?"

"They come in clouds to darken the sun, an' they eat everything in sight. Mostly they like cultivated crops."

Vallian turned his back on her and crossed to his horse. Mounting, he rode away toward the new camp and she stared after him, angry and frustrated.

"He doesn't think much of our chances, does he Ma?" Tom said. "But we'll show him! You just wait!"

"Of course, Tom. Mr. Vallian does not know us, but he has a right to be skeptical. This is a new life for us, and a hard one. We will have to adjust to many changes, I am afraid."

"I hope he stays with us."

"What? What ever put that idea into your head? Why should he stay with us? Mr. Vallian is a drifter, son, so far as we know he just moves from place to place, and from his appearance I would say he doesn't do very well."

"He's been here a long time, I think. And he's alive."

She put her hand on Tom's shoulder. "Yes . . . yes, you are right, Tom. Whatever one might say about him he is alive, and he's able."

Tom kicked dirt into the coals. One after another the coals died out until only a little smoke arose from where the fire had been.

"Come, Tom. We'd better go."

Somewhere an owl hooted, a mournful, lonely sound in the dark trees.

Chapter III

Susanna sat in the darkness near the horses. Tom was beside her, and despite his determination to stay awake, he had fallen asleep at last.

Vallian came to them and spoke softly. "I figure to sleep some. Ma'am, you'd better do the same, like the boy here.

"McKaskel, you take the first watch. Listen, learn the sounds that are natural to the night, and you'll hear most of them in the first hour or so. Any other sound you hear is likely to be them.

"You watch my horse. Those are city horses you've got, so you don't have to pay them much mind. My horse will have his ears up as soon as he hears them coming, and he'll hear them before you do.

"He's mustang—wild stock—and all his young life he had to listen for varmints that might attack him, so he's not likely to miss much. About one o'clock by that watch of yours, you wake me up."

With his saddle for a pillow he lay on his groundsheet and rolled himself in a blanket. Within minutes, he was asleep.

Duncan McKaskel sat down by his wife. "They'll find our fire," he said, "I am sure there will be some smoke. That should take some time, and we may hear them."

"He's a strange man," she said.

"Ssh! He may be awake."

"No, he's breathing evenly. I am sure he's sleeping." After a moment, she added, "We can learn from him, Duncan. He knows so much that we'd better know."

"Yes," he admitted, "I suppose so. The kind of education we have doesn't count for much out here."

After awhile Susanna dozed, and McKaskel got up and moved out, closer to the horses. They were cropping grass in the small circle they had chosen for a camp. For the first time he walked all around it, and shook his head in irritation at himself. He should have seen this place at once. The fallen tree barred all approach from one angle because one end was up against some rocks, the other was near the edge of the bluff. Around that tree there was a good deal of old bark, dried leaves and branches.

Behind them was a thick grove of trees, so thick that a man could push through it only with considerable noise. On the other side were the fallen trees, broken brush and old stumps of a deserted beaver pond. The position was not sheltered from gunfire except near the fallen tree, but it was difficult to find or approach by night.

Vallian had seen the place at once, which indicated how much could be learned by observation. A man had to *see*, not just look.

McKaskel listened, but heard no other sounds than those of the night. He moved carefully, trying to walk without sound, and not to remain in one place too long. He was thinking, trying to understand this new world and to draw on what he remembered from his reading that might help. He sat down on a log and rested, listening.

Several times his eyes almost closed, and after a moment he got up and moved around again, going around the circle of their camp, listening for any new sound. He heard nothing, and when his watch was over he went back to camp and spoke softly to Con Vallian.

The frontiersman was immediately awake. "Time," McKaskel whispered, "and all's quiet."

Vallian sat up and tugged on his boots, slung his gunbelt around his lean hips and took up his rifle. "Get some sleep," he said quietly. "They know you're a tenderfoot and they'll be looking to steal your horses, first. When they don't find them they'll try to get into your camp."

"Wake me. I'll be ready."

Duncan McKaskel stretched out on his blankets. He was tired but he would rest only for a moment. He had to be ready to help, and after all, who was this man to whom they were trusting themselves? He might have plans of his own. Yet even as he thought it he did not accept the idea. He closed his eyes and slept.

A hand on his shoulder awakened him. It was very still. He felt Susanna stir, but although he knew she was awake, she made no sound, listening as he was.

He took up his gun, warning himself that he must be careful not to shoot the wrong man.

Shoot a man? He was startled to realize that he had accepted the idea with no accompanying sense of guilt. Was this what environment did? Or was it his subconscious acceptance of practical necessity?

Susanna watched him move away, then sat up, suddenly aware that Tom was already gone.

Gone? Gone where?

She got up quickly, then stood still, realizing she wore a light-colored dress. Gathering up the blanket that had covered them, she gathered it quickly around her. She had no gun but there was a stout stick nearby, and she knelt down and felt for it. Her hand found it and she straightened up. Something stirred among the leaves near her and she tightened her grip.

There was another faint stir, and then a shadow loomed near, a shorter, broader shadow than either of the men in her camp, wider than her son. Whoever it was had a rancid, unclean odor of one long unbathed.

She gripped the stick, which was about two feet long and a good three inches around, in her two hands. She drew it slowly back. The man was unaware of her, but soon would hear her breathing. She swung the stick at his face with all her strength.

The stick struck with a dull smack, and the man cried out, staggering backward. She struck again, over his head this time, and the man grabbed out frantically, scarcely aware of what he did. Dropping the blanket from her shoulders she thrust the stick at his face and he grabbed it.

Instantly, she kicked out, her foot striking his kneecap. He staggered, lost his grip on the stick and fell. She struck wildly, missed, then hit him again, probably on the arm or shoulder. In the deeper darkness toward the ground she could not see. She was panting with the effort.

Suddenly she heard a shot . . . lighter in sound than Duncan's rifle, then two more. There was a moment of silence, then the heavy bellow of the rifle and silence.

Something was crawling in the brush. For an instant she thought of following, then recovered her blanket and waited where she was.

There was movement from within the camp and someone loomed nearby. The smell this time was of pine and buckskin.

"You all right?" It was Vallian.

"I hit one of them . . . several times."

"Prob'ly more'n we did. What did you hit him with?"

She lifted the stick. "With this. I hit him in the face the first time. With both hands."

She was startled to realize she was speaking with

some pride. What sort of person was she becoming, anyway? "I hit him hard."

He touched the stick. "Reckon you'll do, ma'am. You surely did hit him. There's blood on that stick."

She gasped and let go. The stick fell to the leaves. "I didn't know. I didn't realize—"

"You done just right." Suddenly he said, "Your boy is with the horses. He done all right, too. He was over there holdin' tight to 'em before things started. That's a good boy."

"Duncan? Where is Duncan?"

"He's yonder . . . with the boy. We won't have no more trouble this night. You all should get some sleep."

He moved away in the darkness, leaving emptiness behind. She stood there, holding the blanket around her, feeling the sudden damp chill of the night. Yet she no longer felt secure lying where their bed had been. Taking their canvas groundsheet she drew the bed closer to the wagon.

The wind was stirring, and she looked up. The sky was overcast and the wind rising. The canvas cover on the wagon flapped in the wind.

Duncan came out of the darkness. "Susanna, you'd better sleep in the wagon. I'll sleep under it. It may rain."

She had not liked sleeping alone in the wagon, the space was cramped and she could not see what was happening, but now she was grateful. The darkness was no longer comforting.

"Are you all right, Duncan?"

"Yes, I am. Tom's already under the wagon again."

"Where is *he?*"

"I don't know . . . around somewhere."

"Duncan? I am glad he's here."

He was silent. Was he thinking that she doubted his ability? She had not meant it that way, but two men were better than one.

"So am I," he said quietly.

It was not until she was in the wagon and almost asleep that she realized she had said nothing about hitting that man. She chuckled suddenly. Duncan would be shocked . . . and surprised. After all, a well-brought up young lady did not go around clubbing men in the darkness.

Surprisingly, she slept, and when Duncan touched her arm to awaken her the sky was gray. "Tom's still asleep, but Vallian thinks we should move."

She had not undressed, so she smoothed out her skirt as much as possible and put on her shoes. A fire was going, and Vallian had made coffee. He was squatting near the blaze, warming his hands. He looked around at her. "You look even better in the morning," he said, "Fine thing in a woman."

"What do you know about women in the morning?" she spoke sharply, and without thinking.

"More'n you'd want to hear, I expect. I ain't always lived in the far out lands."

"Are they gone? Those men, I mean?"

"Doubt it. You got too much they want, but the farther out you get the more they'll be likely to leave. Too much chance of Injuns."

"What about us?"

He shrugged. "You seem willin' to take the chance. I've knowed folks to cross all the way without seein' ary an Injun, and others had a fight ever' day. You face things when you get to 'em."

"You don't think we'll make it, do you?"

He shrugged again. "You got a chance."

They ate a quick breakfast and drank coffee. Tom awakened when they were hitching the mules and ate the bacon and bread that had been saved for him.

Con Vallian mounted his horse and took a quick scout through the trees. "Nothin' close by," he said, "Let's roll 'em!"

The wagon moved out, with Duncan handling the mules, his rifle beside him. Tom rode in the back, keeping an eye on the horses. Vallian scouted on ahead.

"I'm sorry to say it," Duncan spoke suddenly, "but there's something about him that irritates me."

"He's a conceited boor."

"Maybe. But he knows this country, Susanna, and he knows how to get along in it. We must take advantage of every minute, and learn from him."

"He moves like a cat."

"Yes . . . yes, he does."

"He said you did very well in the settlement. He spoke well of you."

"He said that?"

They left the trees behind, moved out upon the bald plain. At least, Susanna thought, they can't approach us here without our seeing them. They will have to come out in the open.

Con Vallian had disappeared. She looked around. He was gone—vanished from sight.

"Duncan! What happened? Where did he go?"

He stared, peered around the edges of the wagon cover toward their rear . . . nothing. "Well, I'll be damned!"

Suddenly their wagon topped out on the edge of a long slope. Before them the country was spread out —miles upon miles of pale gray-green grass and exposed ridges of red sandstone. No trees, no brush . . . a few clumps of prickly pear on a slope, and far off a herd of antelope and a few distant black spots.

There, well down the slope before them was Vallian, sitting his horse and looking the country over. Suddenly Susanna was frightened. An army could have hidden here and she would never have guessed . . . or an Indian war party.

Duncan McKaskel drew up and looked out over the wide space before them. They would camp down there tonight, and for days afterward. It was frightening.

He shuddered suddenly, and put his hand on hers. "My God," he said softly, "to think of all that! And if anything happens to us there's nobody to help. There's no doctor, no hospital—"

"We knew it would be that way, Duncan," she said quietly. "We talked about it."

"That's just it. We talked about it. But we did not *know!* There is no way one can know without seeing it, feeling it."

"I wonder how many have died out there? Where nobody knew?"

"Many have died, Susanna, but more will come. There are always people who hope, who wish, who dream."

He gathered the reins and spoke to the mules. They hesitated, leaned into their collars and he slapped them with the reins. The wagon started, and rolled on.

Susanna's eyes went far ahead, to a small, moving dot. He must have turned slightly because the dot went from black to a kind of brown as the sun hit his buckskins.

"We are not quite alone, Duncan," she said quietly. "He is out there. Vallian is there."

"Yes," his eyes were somber, his lips unsmiling. "Yes, he is."

Chapter IV

The "settlement" was a couple of log houses and a barn. In one of the houses there was a bar, a table, and a few crudely-made chairs. Further out there were a few abandoned lean-tos and dugouts. It was in low land near the river, inclined to be swampy.

Doc Shabbitt tilted the jug over his tin cup. He was a fat, sloppy man with small eyes and a mean, petulant mouth.

"They wasn't alone!" he said again. "They had somebody with 'em!"

Dobbs was a thin, dirty man in ragged buckskins. "There was three of them," he insisted. "I scouted their camp, an' we all seen 'em when they come up from the river. It had to be either the woman or the boy who killed Lenny."

"That city woman?" Shabbitt spat. "I'll kill her. If she killed my boy—"

"She's mine." Red Hyle was a powerful man with a sullen look about him. "I done tol' you that. You lay a hand to her before I tell you an' I'll stretch your hide, Doc."

"Now, see here—!"

"You want to argue the question, Doc?" Red Hyle held the bottle poised over his glass, but the bottle was in his left hand. Doc did not want to argue. Nor was it his way to face anything directly. He preferred the oblique. He never expected to have trouble with Red Hyle. He expected to kill him first, but in his own time, when Hyle had something worth killing him for.

Besides, Red was too good with a gun—quick and dangerous.

"You seen the tracks," he said, "he's loaded heavy. He's packin' a lot we could use, an' his stock besides. Those are mighty fine mules."

"I seen a few wagons," Purdy Mantle said, "but none loaded that heavy. I wonder what all he's carryin'?"

"They're well-off. A body can see that."

"Uh-huh . . . so maybe they figure to buy land. Maybe they figure to buy what all they need. That's why their wagon's so heavy."

"What d' you mean, Purdy?" Doc asked.

"Look at it. What's the heaviest thing you know of?"

"Gold?" Ike Mantle stared. "You all figure he's carryin' *gold?*"

"I said no such thing. On'y that wagon's heavy, mighty heavy."

"He killed Lenny," Doc muttered. "He killed my boy."

"Somebody did. Shot right through my hat, too," Ike said. "Lenny would have to be wearin' my hat."

"How's Booster?" Purdy asked.

"He'll carry the scars," Doc said. "His nose is broke, an' he lost some teeth. I'd sure like to know what he was hit with. His face is tore up somethin' awful."

"They was ready for us," Purdy said. "They was settin' waitin'. Who'd figure they'd be all that canny?"

"I tell you," Doc said, "there was somebody else. You look at the tracks around that camp, Purdy?"

"For what? We already knew where they was. I'd no call to go scoutin' around."

"Gold," Ike Mantle said, "supposin' there is gold?"

Nobody spoke for a few minutes. "You all do what you're of a mind to," Red Hyle said, "I'm follerin'. That there's a woman. I ain't seen anythin' like her since those fancy rich women from up on the hill at Natchez."

"We lost nothin' here," Doc agreed. "I'm ready to get shut of this place. Leave it for the next outfit, just like we found it."

Red Hyle got to his feet and walked out. For a moment there was silence, and then Purdy said, "He's really got woman on his mind."

"Did you see her?" Doc said.

"I saw her. But I wouldn't get myself killed for her. Not me."

Purdy Mantle was the last one to leave, finishing off the bottle, then throwing it into a corner where it shattered to bits. He followed the others outside, leaning against the wall and thinking. Lenny Shabbitt was dead, and he was no loss, but it had been passed over that he was wearing Ike's hat. Maybe whoever killed Lenny had wanted to kill Ike . . . and there were a lot who would take pleasure in it.

Purdy looked down at his scuffed boots. He ought to get away from them. He should get shut of them now and go his own way.

Ike, too. Ike was as bad as the worst of them, because Ike was mean . . . downright mean. Brother he might be, but he was a mean, cruel man. He felt no love for his younger brother, nor did Ike feel any for him. They'd been born to the same parents but they were far apart in everything else.

Now they were going to follow after that tenderfoot and his family. Purdy hitched up his gun. He was better with a gun than any of them, unless it was Red Hyle. He'd often wondered about that.

He had seen Hyle shoot, and he had seen only one man he thought was as good . . . just one.

He'd seen Con Vallian down in the Bald Knob country that time, and Con was quick. He was almighty quick at a time when a man was either quick or he was dead.

Ike came up, leading their horses. "Saddled up for you." Ike squinted at him. "You draggin' your feet, Purd?"

"Lazy," Purdy said, "lazy in the sun."

"You think too much. Thinkin' never got a man any place. You start to study on things and all you get is mixed up."

"I was thinkin' about Red Hyle."

Ike shot him a quick look. "Wonderin' was you as slick as him? Don't you try it, Purd. What if you was? You'd get yourself shot up for no good reason. He gives you trouble, just shoot him . . . or I will. Don't call him out."

There were eight of them when they rode out of the settlement bound west. Doc Shabbitt, who thought he was the leader and the brains. Red Hyle, who rode with them but was not one of them, Ike and Purdy Mantle, Johnny Dobbs who was a wanted man somewhere back east, Booster McCutcheon, who was in no shape to ride but had no choice but ride or be left, Boston Pangman, and the Huron.

Nobody knew whether the Huron was really a Huron or not. Somehow or other he had drifted in with them and somebody called him Huron. He wore white man's clothes and talked a poor white man's tongue, but he was dark enough to be an Indian. He was a good man in the woods, and could handle a canoe or boat. What else he could do they did not know . . . or care.

The sun was high when they started west, but they were in no hurry. The plains were wide and long. A wagon with four mules and a heavy load does not move very fast, so they'd take their own time. Besides, the deeper into prairie country they were the less chance of their crime being discovered or revealed.

In camp the firelight flickered. Out upon the prairie the grass was a white sea under the high, pale moon. There was a smell of sun-ripened grass and cooling water. There was a smell of wood-smoke and bacon frying, and beside the fire three people bound westward.

"It has been three days," Susanna said. "I think he has left us."

"Well? Why not? What duty has he to us?"

He had none, of course, yet there was an empty place at coffee-time, and a voice they did not hear in their quiet talking.

"Do you think the others will come after us?"

"He thought so," Tom said. "He told me I must listen. That I must always listen."

Their days had been measured by creeks, some dry, some with a trickle of water, a few running strong and well. Prairie Chicken Creek, Rock Creek, Elm Creek. They had made good time, twenty miles each day, and the turf had been firm even though their wheel-tracks still cut deep.

"Pa? The mules are sure gaunt. They are not eating tonight . . . just standing."

"They need rest, Tom. We should stop for a day, let them catch up."

Susanna straightened from the fire, a fork in her hand. "Duncan? Do we dare?"

"We will have to. We can't escape them, anyway. They can travel further in two days than we can in five if they wish to. It will serve no good purpose to kill our stock. I'd like to get further along, but maybe it is better here. This is a good spring."

He felt better today for he had killed an antelope, their first fresh meat. They broiled some of it over the fire and ate well.

"Susanna? I saw some tracks today."

"His?"

"No . . . unshod ponies. They were Indian tracks, quite a few of them. They were dragging their tent-poles like Indians do."

Susanna took the first watch. There were only the three of them now, and her husband and her son needed all the rest they could get. At seven o'clock when the dishes were all put away and only the cof-fee-pot left on the fire, she took her rifle and went out to the edge of camp.

She had found a place there where some low rocks and brush covered the top of a knoll. She sat down among them and let the darkness close in around her. On her right and below she could see the faint wink-ing eye of the campfire, and the shadow of the once-white wagon-top.

It was very still. The moon was bright, yet al-ready it had started descending toward the horizon. Long before Duncan succeeded Tom on watch the moon would be gone. Nothing moved out there. At least, nothing she could see. She thought of home and wondered what her sisters were doing now.

It would not be late back there. Dinner would be almost over unless they had gone out or were enter-taining. The lights would be bright along the streets, people would be sitting out in porch-swings and talk-ing, while some of the young people would be gath-ered around a piano, singing.

Far off, a coyote howled . . . then another. Or was it a wolf?

Something stirred down below and a shadow moved in front of their fire. She frowned, half-rising. Dun-can must be awake . . . she knew he never felt easy with her out alone and on watch . . . yet, he should be asleep. Tom certainly would be. Tom was a good sleeper, although he awakened early, as Duncan did.

"Quiet tonight."

The voice froze her with horror. She had seen noth-ing, heard nothing.

She started to rise, but a hand on her shoulder

held her down. "No need to get up. I just came out to keep you comp'ny."

It was Con Vallian.

"You! Mr. Vallian, you—"

"Surprised you, huh? Figured I would, an' good for you. Keeps you from gettin' too sure of yourself, an' that can be fatal out here. On'y ones who can be sure of theirselves is the dead."

"Where have you been?"

"Missed me, did you? Well, I been circulatin'. Don't do for a man to get in a rut, now, does it? I been seein' some country but I figured you all'd be needin' me."

"We did miss you, Mr. Vallian. After all, you've been a big help to us."

"I missed you, too. Missed your coffee, so I went down an' had me a cup."

"You were in *camp?*" She was horrified.

"Yes, ma'am, I surely was. But don't you worry, I didn't wake anybody, and didn't bother 'em. I just had me some coffee and broiled some of that there antelope."

"You mean you actually cooked some meat? You actually—"

"Yes'm. I actually. You folks sleep pretty good these nights. Fresh air and weariness will do it ever' time."

"You . . . you could have killed them!"

"Yes'm. I reckon so. But don't you worry none. Shabbitt ain't that good an Injun. About those others I'm not so sure. Ike Mantle maybe is."

"I thought you killed him. Wasn't he the one?"

"A man can make a mistake. I figured there wasn't two hats like that anywhere about, so when I fetched a bullet into that one I reckoned it was Ike. Must have been Doc Shabbitt's son though. He had him a no-account boy about nineteen or twenty."

"That's too young to die. I am sorry for him."

"Too young to die? Any time is, when you think on it. Sorry for him? Well, I ain't. He was born mean an' he was raised mean, an' he had his rifle pointed right at your husband's back. He was surely plannin' to kill him, only my bullet stopped him and I guess it jolted him off target. At that distance he wouldn't have missed."

"Why did you come back?"

He chuckled. "Oh, I figured I'd like to see how you folks handle Injuns. You're about to meet up with a passel of them."

"Indians? You mean we'll be attacked?"

"Maybe, maybe not. You can never tell about Injuns, ma'am, they have notions of their own."

"When?"

"They'll come in about sun-up, I guess, to see how wide awake you are. There'll be maybe a dozen or so."

"What will they do?"

"Depends on you folks."

She stood up. "It is time for me to awaken Duncan."

He got up too. He looked down at her, and she knew he was grinning that exasperating grin. "You sure you want to go in? You right sure?"

She looked up at him and said quite calmly, "Yes, Mr. Vallian, I am sure."

She turned away and walked a dozen steps before she turned to look back. "I am sure of something else, too, Mr. Vallian."

"Yeah? What's that?"

"I am sure that you are a gentleman, Mr. Vallian."

Chapter V

Before the sun appeared the earth was still, and silence lay like a blessing upon the land. No blade stirred in the coolness, nor any bird in the sky, only somewhere not too far off, a meadow lark spoke inquiringly into the morning.

One arresting finger of smoke lifted thinly to the sky, and where the horizon drew its line across the heavens, a cloud seemed to lie upon the grass, off where the world curved away from them.

"Put everything away," Vallian advised, "put your goods out of sight. You've got a-plenty of flour and sugar, so plan to spare them some."

"We've scarcely enough to make it through," Susanna protested.

"Take out a third," Vallian said, "but don't let it show. An' remember this: don't look scared. Injuns got no respect for a frightened man. You got to make them stand first, then give them something. If they figure you're scared they'll just take it all an' you scalps, too."

"I don't see anybody," Tom protested. "Ain't no-body in sight for miles."

"Shut up, boy, an' listen." After a moment he said, "Trouble with city folks. Always talkin'. You never learn anything when you're talkin', boy, only when you're listenin'."

The clouds flushed pink, and a streak of bright crimson slashed the sky, reflecting on the grass and giving it a rosy sheen.

"Shouldn't we be moving?" McKaskel asked, irrita-bly. "Why wait like this? How do you know there is anyone out there?"

"I know. They're watchin' us." Vallian paused. "You got a Bible?"

"A Bible. Of course."

"Get it out, stand there in front of us an' read. Read, an' take in the sky an' all. The Injuns," he added, "may not buy it, but they like a good show."

Duncan McKaskel went to the wagon and got his Bible. He straightened his coat, stretched his neck out of his collar. He walked out and faced them. "I think this is nonsense," he said, self-consciously. "And I am no minister of the gospel."

"Right this minute," Con Vallian removed his hat, "you surely are. You're a gospel-shoutin', fire an' brim-stone preacher. Now when they come, don't none of you turn a hair. Pay them no mind."

McKaskel opened the Bible and turned the pages. Suddenly from behind him there were shrill, piping yells. Involuntarily, he started to turn.

"Read!" Vallian spoke sharply. "Read, if you want to live!"

Behind him there were pounding hoofs, and the wild, shrill yells. He read, *"For the waters of Nimrum shall be desolate: For the hay is withered away, the rass faileth, there is no green thing."*

He paused just a moment and he saw Susanna's e go pale. The horses were thundering down upon n and suddenly they halted, dust drifted forward and over them, and he could smell the hot sweat smell of horses, and he could hear their gasping right behind him, and he continued to read, *"Therefore the abundance they have gotten, and that which they have laid up, shall they carry away to the brook of willows."*

Slowly he turned to face the Indians. His heart was pounding, but he said quietly, "Would you care to join us?" he gestured at the ground around him, and indicated they should be seated, but one Indian, with a strongly-hewn face and an eagle beak of a nose said, "No! We are hungry! You must feed us!" He waved his coup stick in the air.

Susanna spoke softly, "Duncan? Maybe—"

"No!" Con Vallian's hat was still in his hand, held near his belt, in his left hand. "We will give you nothing! There is meat out there! The Arapaho are great hunters! Let them hunt!"

The warrior's eyes turned to Vallian, measuring him with care, then to Duncan McKaskel, who had lowered his Bible to his side. He stood close to the wagon, and there was a rifle there, ready at hand.

"We are hungry," the warrior spoke harshly. "What you have, we will take!"

"Our wagon is small," Vallian said, "and not worth the warriors who must die to take it. If you wish to come, then come, but sing your death-songs before you do, for many will die."

He lowered his hat, and in his hand he held a gun.

"Mac," he said quietly, "put the book on the tailgate of the wagon and take up your rifle. Keep your eyes on 'em, but do it slow.

"Tom?" he spoke a little louder. "Show 'em your piece. Just show 'em . . . don't shoot."

The muzzle of the gun came through the drawstrings at the rear of the wagon.

"We come in peace. We do not stop in your land, but we have little food, less than we need to get where we go, and the Arapaho are hunters, great hunters."

The warrior waved a hand over the country. "There is no game. We have killed nothing. We are hungry. Our papooses are hungry."

Vallian spoke again. "You have young ones? How many are they?"

"Nine?" The warrior held up nine fingers, hesitantly.

"Mrs. McKaskel, go to your wagon and get out twenty pounds of flour, as near as you can get to it, and put out a little salt, some sugar, and that haunch of antelope."

"It is starting to spoil," she protested.

"Makes no mind. You lay it out. Half the meat they eat is spoilin'."

She did so, working swiftly. She brought the meat, flour, sugar, and salt to the Indians and placed the packages on the ground.

"We have no war with the Arapaho, who are brave men and great warriors. We cannot feed warriors, but we will not see your children grow thin and cry in the night for hunger.

"Take this for your children, and go with God. Walk with the Great Spirit upon the good grass, and be not worried."

Duncan McKaskel spoke suddenly. "Be not worried," he repeated, "the buffalo will come, and the antelope. You will hunger no more."

The Indians dismounted, took up the food, and wheeled and dashed off, leaving only dust behind. They raced away, vanishing over a low line of hills, and Duncan McKaskel turned and stared at Susanna.

Her face was white, and she was trembling. She looked at Con Vallian. "Would they have killed us?"

"Likely. Like I said, Indians are notional. Stand up to 'em and they like you, knuckle under and you're beneath contempt, lower than a dog's belly."

"That was kind of you, to think of their children."

Vallian shrugged. "Kind, hell! I was thinkin' of my scalp. Injuns think a sight of their young uns, and offerin' to feed them taken us off the hook."

"I didn't know you had that gun."

"Out here you better have a gun, and a gun in the wagon ain't good for nothin'. I believe what the old Quaker said, 'Trust in the Lord, but keep your powder dry.' "

Swiftly, they harnessed the team and moved out on the plains. Before them, not over a mile away, they saw a wooded creek.

Vallian pointed. "Stop there an' load up with wood. You'll be needin' it. Your next stop is Lost Spring, sixteen, seventeen miles west, an' there's nothing there, nothing but a few buffalo chips, far out on the prairie. Everything close by has been used."

"What about the Indians?"

"If they want you, they'll find you. I say load up with fuel. From here on you'd better sling a canvas underneath your wagon. Let your wife an' boy walk behind an' pick up buffalo chips—"

"*Pick* them up? With our *hands?*"

"Yes, ma'am. They're dry . . . if you're careful which ones you pick, an' they'll be the only fuel you'll have for miles. You sling that canvas underneath and when they pick up the chips they can toss them into the canvas along with any sticks they can find. You'll be needin' fuel."

The sun was up now, although just above the horizon. The sky had hazed over and a wind kicked sudden gusts that flapped their canvas top and blew the horses' manes.

Duncan McKaskel walked beside his mules, and Vallian rode close to the wagon seat, near Susanna. "That was a good thought, he had," Vallian commented, "telling them the buffalo would come. Injuns set store by medicine men. Him carrying on with the Bible like that . . . they'll think he's a preacher."

"And if the buffalo do not come?"

Vallian chuckled. "Now, ma'am, that never unsettled no medicine man, nor preacher, either! He can just say it was their fault, that there was sin in their village, that there was no faith."

"You are a cynic."

"No, ma'am, but when a miracle doesn't come off you don't just expect to set by, do you? You got to have a reason. Sin's the reason they'll buy . . . you can just bet, ma'am, that somebody was doing something he shouldn't have, so they'll blame him, not the prophet."

"Why did they charge us like that?"

"Scarin' you. Seein' if you had backbone. They weren't a war party . . . just travelin' with their folks. You got to judge them according to their lights, ma'am. Injuns think different than us, but that doesn't say they are wrong . . . just different."

"It would have taken all we had to feed them! Why, there must have been a dozen of them!"

"No, ma'am, there was eight, but when it comes to Injuns that's too many. They'd have taken all you had, then searched your wagon. If you'd let 'em have it all, they'd have taken it all and everything else they wanted, but when we stood fast and showed our guns, they were willin' to talk. They're good folks, ma'am, but they just don't think like we do. You got to allow for that."

Twice they stopped to rest the mules. At their nooning, Duncan said, "Susanna, I think you and Tom had better walk some more. The mules are making hard work of it."

"Throw out that chest," Vallian said, "or the dresser. You're going to kill them mules."

"I will do no such thing!" Susanna said sharply. "Why, the very idea! My grandmother owned that dresser! She had it from her husband's mother. Why, it's been in our family for years and years!"

"Maybe," Vallian commented dryly, "but it sure won't pull your wagon when those mules are played out, and the way you're usin' 'em those mules won't last another week . . . maybe ten days. And in ten days, ma'am, you just aren't going to be anywhere. Not anywhere at all!"

Lost Spring was nowhere. It was bald prairie all around, not a stick of wood, not even a buffalo chip. There was not a bush or a tree anywhere within sight. During the night the wind blew hard and before daylight it began to rain. It was a spitting, doubtful rain at first, then after an interlude, a brisk but brief shower.

Duncan led the mules to water, then the horses. Tom helped to make camp. It was not easy in the rain. Vallian scooped out a small hollow in the earth, gathered a few stones, and using dry wood from the tarp slung under the wagon, he got a fire going.

With a canvas over the fire they broiled some antelope steaks and ate their small meal and drank coffee standing in the rain.

"How far to the next camp?" Tom asked.

"Sixteen miles . . . maybe a shade less. There's wood there, and grass. It's a good camp."

"Well, that will be a help. At least, we can pick up some more wood tomorrow."

"Not you."

They turned their heads to stare at him. Vallian returned the look. "You ain't goin' to be there tomorrow. Maybe not the next day."

"What do you mean?" Susanna demanded sharply.

"Your mules are tuckered. They just made it to here, and when you come in it was dry. Tomorrow those wheels will be cuttin' into mud. With luck you'll make that camp on Cottonwood Creek in three days."

"Three days! For sixteen miles?"

"Maybe not even then. Maybe not at all."

Tom's face was white, and for a moment Susanna thought she would cry. Duncan stared then looked at the ground, feeling empty and sick.

"I don't believe that," he said, "we'll make it."

"If the mules die," Vallian said, "you can always ride out on the horses. Of course, you can't carry much. An' you surely can't carry that dresser."

He emptied his cup. "See that hill yonder? Tomorrow you'll start fresh. You'll roll down the slope pretty well, then you'll start up. If you make it to the top, that's where you'll camp tomorrow night."

"That's ridiculous! Why, that's no more than six or seven hundred yards!"

"That's right. And maybe you won't even get out of the valley. I told you, mister, you're fixin' to kill them mules."

Vallian walked to his horse. "You'll be needin' meat. I'll ride out."

"Mr. Vallian?" Tom asked suddenly. "Can I come with you? I can shoot."

"I've got no time for youngsters. You stay with your ma."

Susanna spoke quickly. "Mr. Vallian, my son must learn to hunt. Won't you teach him?"

He started to refuse, a foot in the stirrup. Then he swung into the saddle. "All right . . . saddle up."

"Thank you, Mr. Vallian," Susanna said.

"Don't thank me. If he can't keep up, he'll get lost. If he comes back with meat it'll be his doin', not mine."

Susanna stared at him. "I do not think I like you, Mr. Vallian."

He smiled, slowly, exasperatingly. "No, ma'am. I reckon not. But then it doesn't matter very much, does it?"

They rode away, and she stared after him, then stamped her foot. It made no sound on the wet grass and that made her even angrier.

Chapter VI

Con Vallian rode straight away from the wagon without turning to look back. His eyes swept the long grass levels, alert for movement or change in the grass. Tom McKaskel rode one of the sorrels, a larger, stronger horse than Vallian's mustang.

In the distance a rainstorm marched across the flatland. There seemed no break in the vast level of the prairie. Thunder rumbled.

"Not a good time for hunting," Vallian commented. "Game holes up when it rains."

Tom was silent. They knew little of this man who had come so suddenly from nowhere, and who seemed to have no ties, no loyalty but to himself and what he believed. Yet there was a strength in him and an awareness that fascinated Tom.

"Buffalo can't hide, an' we're cuttin' sign in buffalo country."

"Will those men come back?"

"Likely."

"You don't think much of us, do you?"

"I don't think about you at all. You come out here loaded like you was going to a city market. You got enough on that wagon for four, five families. Your pa ought to have more sense."

"Pa knows what he's doing."

"Back east, maybe. What you learn in school cuts no ice out here. You started out to get across the plains. Well, you got no choice now. You're on your way an' the only way you're going to make it is by chucking half your load."

"Half!"

"Boy, you keepin' your eyes open?"

"Sure I am! Why,—"

Tom felt guilty. To tell the truth he had been arguing and not paying attention. Now he looked quickly around.

"You got no time to study out here. You see, and you act. Only you don't shoot at movement. You never squeeze off your shot until you know exactly what you're shootin' at. Tenderfeet, they shoot at anything that moves. They kill cows, horses, dogs an' each other.

"Out here we kill just what we need to live, just like a wolf does, or a bear. Not to say they won't kill once in awhile just to be killin', but they're animals, boy, you're a man . . . or about to be one.

"Look yonder . . . see anything?"

"No, I . . . well, there's something dark, right close to the ground."

"Them's buffalo, an' they ain't close to the ground, they're feedin' in a hollow or gully. But we ain't huntin' buffalo right now. Your pa'd try to carry the hide, and he ought. Trouble is buffalo hides weigh heavy, mighty heavy, an' you have more truck on that wagon than the Israelites fleein' Egypt."

Vallian reined his horse around, glancing at the grass. "Injuns," he said, " and the same ones."

Tom looked, but the plain before them was empty. Vallian pointed at the grass, some distance ahead.

"There! Where the grass has been pressed down. They passed by here, heading west."

Tom could see nothing but as they rode nearer he could distinguish a difference in the shade of the grass, and then he could see that some of the grass had been pressed down. The two lines left by the travois were clearly indicated.

Another travois had dragged along, almost in the same tracks as the first.

"Fifteen, anyway. We seen eight bucks an' there would be some women and kids."

"How can you tell?"

"Boy, anybody can see that. They passed after dew-fall. You got to keep your eyes open. You can't just ride along lookin' at pretty colors like your pa does."

"My pa's all right. You leave him out of this or say it to his face, and if you do, you'd better think twice. He was a boxer in school."

"I seen some o' them boxers. I whupped one down to Natchez one time. Your pa's all right, boy, only he's come west with a wife and child, and if he's wishful of keepin' them alive he's got to learn new ways. New ways of thinkin', mostly."

He led the way down the slope. "We ain't after buffalo, so we'll just amble along. We should fetch up some antelope soon." He wiped his mouth with the back of his hand. "I seen 'em come an' go. I been ridin' this land since I was half your size, fightin' Injuns an' huntin' with em—"

"You fight them and yet you're friendly with them?"

"Why not? Nobody fights all the time. We've fought a time or two, an' good fights they were, too. Sometimes we set over a fire and talk of the fool mistakes we made, or almost made. Not that you get a chance to make many mistakes when you're fightin' Injuns."

He pointed suddenly. "There! Pronghorns . . . must be fifteen to twenty of them. Come on, we'll circle around and come up downwind of them . . . but we got to stay out of sight, too, because they can see."

He rode down the slope ahead of Tom, a tall man, easy in the saddle. The mustang was smaller than the sorrel, but quick. The horse moved easily, taking the opposite slope as if it were not there, riding across the back of the knoll where they had seen the antelope.

At the crest of the low ridge he drew up, and then edged his horse closer until he could see over the top of the hill. The antelope were no more than one hundred yards away. He backed off, dismounted, and edged forward. Lifting his rifle he held on his target for a long instant until Tom thought he would never fire. Suddenly the rifle leaped in his hands, but instantly he shifted his muzzle a few inches and fired again.

Before moving he extracted the two cartridges and fed two more into the rifle. Letting Tom lead his horse, he walked up to the crest of the rise. Both antelope were down, the rest of the herd disappearing in the distance.

"Keep your eyes open, boy," Vallian said sharply, "and don't do no moon-gazin'. If you see anything move, even the grass, you speak out, d'you hear?

"If you're goin' to live in this country you got to learn that you don't cover country by just settin' up on a horse. You keep your eyes open or some Injun'll be settin' on the horse and you'll be dead."

"Mr. Vallian? Couldn't you have gone around that knob yonder and come up closer to them? To the antelope, I mean?"

"Boy, you listen now. Once an antelope sees you, you've either got to shoot, or try movin' up right at him, straight and slow. If an antelope sees something, then sees it disappear, he'll be gone. When we'd have come out from behind that knob they'd be a mile off an' travelin'.

"An antelope has eyes like a field glass. He lives on these prairies and he knows 'em, his eyes are made for seeing long distances. He can hear, too. You can stalk a deer, but you don't get much chance with an antelope.

"They are all curious, almighty curious. You can lie up and toll 'em right up to you with a slow moving cloth on a ramrod or something that shines or sparkles. You can even get 'em close with a bare hand or foot, wiggling your fingers or toes."

"They make a track like a deer."

Vallian spat. "No more like a deer than mine's like yours. To a tenderfoot, maybe. Antelope track is shorter than a deer track, broader and rounder at the heel, an' sharp at toe. You study 'em. You'll be able to tell the dif'rence."

Tom's eyes kept turning, studying the prairie all around. Vallian was a hard man, and he did not want to draw his anger, for obviously he was impatient with ignorance and poor observation.

"Could you teach me to be a frontiersman?" he asked suddenly. "I'd like to learn."

"I ain't running no school. You keep your eyes open, watch what you're about and if you live long enough you'll learn, but you'll keep on learning. There's no end to it, boy. I've lived all my life on the frontier and I don't know the half of it.

"The trouble is, this here's a school where the Injuns conduct the examinations. Injuns or the wild country itself."

"You skinned only one antelope."

"That's right, boy. I'll shoot meat for 'em when they're in trouble, but I'll be damned if I'll skin it, too."

"Them?"

Vallian gave him a disgusted glance. "Injuns, boy. Them Injuns we seen the other night. Now you keep your rifle in your hands. Don't wave it around, just hold it easy-like."

"I don't see any—"

There were three of them, and they rode out of a coulee Tom had not even seen, and drew up, facing them. Vallian gestured at the antelope lying on the grass, then pointed with his forefinger, bent it and drew it to him as if hooking something in. "Means 'take' or 'catch,'" he said. "In the tribe Indians share their meat."

"Are we in their tribe now?" Tom asked.

"If they were a war party they'd kill you just as soon as they'd a chance. No, we ain't of their tribe, but they need meat. They'd share what they had with us, even though they might take our scalps after."

They rode slowly away, and Tom turned his head to stare back. The Indians were cutting up the meat, paying no attention to them. After a bit Vallian started to lope his horse.

Suddenly, Vallian said, "Boy, awhile back you stuck up for your pa. That's good. I like loyalty in a man."

"He's a good man," Tom said.

"I reckon he is, or your ma wouldn't have married him. Some women I'd not say that of, but your ma is a canny woman. You listen to your folks, boy. They'll learn you right. 'Cept about injuns and wild country. Then you listen to me."

Now they could see the white top of the wagon. It was where they had left it, and they could see the lift of smoke from the fire.

"You pa, now, does he know all about them old Greeks? Achilles, an' them?"

"Yes, he does. He can read Greek."

"Sure enough? I reckon that keeps him right busy out here, doesn't it?" They were nearing the wagon. "You know them stories, boy? About all that killin' an' fightin'?"

"I know some of it. Pa knows it very well." Tom was suddenly curious. "Do you know those stories?"

"Used to hear 'em, long time back." He hesitated.

They rode up to the fire.

"Ma!" Tom was excited. "Mr. Vallian killed two antelopes, and we met those Indians again!"

Duncan accepted the meat Vallian handed him,

and glanced at it. "That's not much meat for two antelopes, Vallian."

"I left one for the Injuns," Vallian did not look around as he uncinched and removed his saddle.

"That was kind of you, Mr. Vallian," Susanna said.

Vallian looked at her. "I didn't think kind, ma'am, I just left it."

Chapter VII

Doc Shabbitt studied the tracks, then glanced over at the Huron. "What do you make of it?"

The Huron said nothing. He rode his horse in a small circle, studying the tracks. "There is another one," he said, "a man who rides alone."

"If he's with them he surely ain't ridin' alone," Ike commented.

"He is not always with them. He rides up, he rides away. He was not with them many miles back, and he rode up to them from the west."

"Who d' you reckon?" Booster asked.

"Aw, it's just some Injun, beggin' flour! We cut their sign back a ways."

"I don't like it," Purdy said quietly, "whoever shot Lenny must be around somewhere, and I don't think it was that woman or the boy. I think somebody else is in this."

"Injuns," Ike insisted. "Why would he ride off thataway? Those Injuns are not far off and one rides over now and again to beg . . . maybe fixin' to kill the lot of them. We surely ain't the first to see those horses nor that woman."

"Injuns don't care what a woman looks like," Ike scoffed. "They don't care one bit."

"Neither do you, Ike," Boston Pangman said, grinning. "I remember a time or two—"

Ike looked around. "You got a big mouth, Pang. You surely do."

Boston Pangman looked at him, then shut up. After a minute he said, "I was just funnin', Ike. No offense."

Ike Mantle said nothing. He rode around, studying the tracks, and then without a word started off along the trail. Doc Shabbitt scowled, then followed him, riding a little faster to get ahead.

If a man was a leader, he had to lead. Ike had no business starting off like that, but then, Ike paid no attention to anyone or anything.

Doc Shabbitt glanced around at the others who were now following. He rubbed his horse's neck. "I'd like to get shut of this bunch," he said aloud.

The riders closed in around him. "They'll be on the Arkansas," Dobbs said. "We'll come up to them there."

"He's well-fixed," Booster said. "No man goes out on the prairie with a load like that unless it's valuable. He's got mules, and they cost twice to three times what oxen cost, and them's good horses. Matched sorrels like that, you can make yourself a deal with them."

"Maybe just women's stuff," Purdy argued. "We don't know that he's got anything worth the trouble. You know how womenfolks are."

"I know how they are," Doc Shabbitt said. "I really do."

"You wait an' see," Purdy insisted. "They wouldn't be carrying gold. Folks come out here to get it, they don't bring it with them. All they'll have will be women's fixin's."

"You figure that if you want," Doc Shabbitt said. "I think there's gold in that wagon."

Red Hyle had said nothing. He was slouched in the saddle, just letting them talk. Purdy glanced at him. What about that now? Was he as fast as Red? Sure. He'd never seen anybody he couldn't out-draw. But supposing, just supposing, that he was not? Supposing it came to a showdown and Red *was* faster?

He'd be dead.

The mules had lost weight, but they were still pulling. So far the prairies had been soft only in spots and the wagon had moved well, but they were climbing steadily. Not much, just barely enough to feel, but the mules knew it. So did they, when they got down and walked . . . and these days they walked most of the time.

The road had improved, and the drive to Cottonwood Creek had been only sixteen miles, although the grade was noticeable and the grass had been good. They had arrived early and the mules had time to graze comfortably before being brought in close for the night. The following day the drive had been long and hard, but there, too, at Turkey Creek, the grass was good. There was no fuel and they cooked with buffalo chips and wood brought from earlier camps.

On the first day Con Vallian had disappeared, riding off with only a wave of the hand. Nor did they see him again during their camps at Cottonwood or Turkey Creeks. Susanna found her eyes constantly seeking for him. "I wonder where he is?" she asked suddenly. "Where does he camp?"

"There's no telling. He's like an Indian, Susanna. One day he will ride off and we will not see him again."

"I suppose so."

Tom turned toward them from the back of the wagon. "He thinks those men . . . the ones back at the settlement . . . he thinks they are following us."

"I doubt it," Duncan said, "they'd not follow us this far."

"We killed one of them," Susanna said. "Maybe they are vengeful men."

"It's hard to believe," Duncan McKaskel stared at the horizon, "there was actually a man killed. Why, I never even saw a man killed before! Come to think of it, I did not see that one killed."

"He was trying to kill you."

"I know . . . although that hardly seems real. I wonder if he really was? Or did Vallian shoot him for reasons of his own?"

"They had your horses, Pa. They threatened you."

"Yes," he admitted reluctantly, "yes, they did, but when it comes to killing . . . well, I doubt if—"

"You said you felt the bullet's wind when it passed you. You heard the sound of it."

"I know," Duncan was having second thoughts, and violence was no part of his ordered plan for living. "But I've heard that if a bullet is fired nearby the report is sometimes heard a second time if you're standing near a tree or post. I could have been mistaken."

"There was no mistake about the man I hit," Susanna said, rather sharply. "He was an armed man and he was creeping up to our camp. I hit him, and I'm glad."

Duncan laughed. "I had no idea you were so warlike."

"One does what one has to," she said simply. "I've begun to realize that the world is not made up of nice, well-mannered people. There are those, of course, but there are others. Back east we had the law to restrain them, out here we have nothing."

"It's up to us," Tom said quietly. "That's what Con Vallian says."

Twice they stopped to rest the horses, and Susanna looked carefully around before they started on. She was alarmed at the change in the mules. They had lost flesh and looked gaunt and tired.

They nooned near a brushy gully and they all took

time to pick up sticks to put in the tarp slung under the wagon. Duncan led the mules to water, then let them graze on the buffalo grass nearby.

The air was very still, the sky impossibly clear. Susanna walked slowly toward a small knoll and climbed it. There were a few rocks there, and after a glance around for snakes, she sat down. The wind blew gently against her face and stirred her hair.

She realized with a sort of shock that she loved this country and when Tom came up the hill to join her, she said as much.

"I do, too, Ma. I like to look away there for miles and see all that land. It's marvelous."

"It is very mountainous where we're going, Tom. It won't be like this."

"Do you think those men are following us?"

She hesitated. There was no purpose in lying. When trouble came, he must face it too. "Yes, Tom, I think they are. I think Mr. Vallian was right and that they are very bad men. Your father doesn't like to admit it to himself, he has such faith in people, but he believes it, too."

"Will we have to fight?"

"I think so. Unless we find some other people . . . good people."

"Out here? I think we had better get ready to fight."

She got up, and they stood there a moment, looking at the vast space. And then, far off—

Tom spoke first. "Ma! Somebody's coming. See?" He pointed. "Away yonder where that draw comes into the plain."

It was only a dot, a speck in all that vastness, as they watched the speck grew, and was accompanied by a small cloud of dust.

"It's Vallian," Susanna said. "Nobody sits a horse quite like him."

Tom strained his eyes, but could not make him out. Only a man and a horse drawing nearer.

"We'd better go down," she said, "Pa is hitching up the team."

They walked down the hill together, and Susanna saw that Duncan had both his shotgun and rifle near the seat, but she made no comment except to mention Vallian's approach.

They moved out, walking beside the team, and a few minutes later Con Vallian skirted the trees near their last camp and rode up the slight grade.

"Figured you might need some help," he said dryly, "with the unloading."

"Unloading?"

"Uh-huh. Right ahead of you is some sand-hills. You're going to have to get shut of that load there or kill them mules. Arkansas River's not far from here."

"We'll manage," McKaskel spoke stiffly, resenting the assurance in Vallian's tone. "My mules can handle it."

"Mighty fine mules," Vallian agreed, "ain't quite as pert as they was. Reckon it's the climate?"

He rode on ahead, and Duncan stared after him. "That man—! I wish he'd—!"

"Don't say it, Duncan. He has helped us, and he will again."

Yet when the mules leaned into the harness and strained to start the wagon, he felt guilty. They were pulling too hard. It was stupidity to continue on in this way, and his own stubbornness was at fault. For some time he had known they must discard something . . . but what?

Susanna loved her furniture. The bed they might keep, but that chiffonier. . . .

He could see the drift-sand ahead.

"We can hitch the sorrels ahead of the mules. They aren't draft animals but they can do it. They've been driven to a light wagon."

Twice in the next quarter of a mile, they stopped. It was then he went to the wagon and looked for the other sets of harness. The extra harnesses had been brought along for repairs, and he had little idea of actually working the sorrels. He got the harness out and threw it on the horses, glancing into the wagon as he did so. The sheen of the mahogany made him turn his head. He was irritated by his feeling of guilt.

They moved forward again, with Tom walking ahead, trying to scout the best route among the sandhills. Even with the horses the load was heavy.

Before them were the breaks of the Arkansas, a rough, wooded and brushy area where any danger might lurk. Emerging into a small open space they found three graves. From the brief words scratched on the crosses two had died from cholera, one from Indians.

Vallian noticed them, and shrugged. "Riding back from Californy I counted more'n a thousand graves of folks that died or were killed last year."

His amusement was ironic. "I reckon some of them tried to go through to the gold fields with their wagons loaded too heavy."

"Possibly," Duncan said quietly, "possibly they did just that. And perhaps some of them managed to get through, even though they were over-loaded."

"Mr. Vallian, were you ever married?"

"Me? Never."

"Women, Mr. Vallian, often build their lives around things. The proper things in their proper places give women assurance, a sense of rightness and stability. Perhaps we men lack that, for better or worse, or maybe we have other things to which we give our attention.

"In this wagon we have a bed that my wife's family brought over from Devonshire almost two hundred years ago. We have several other articles of furniture equally as important. We could very easily have left those articles at home and loaded the space with food or implements, but the happiness of Susanna is very important to me, and wherever we are, those things will be home to her. Do you understand, Mr. Vallian?"

Con pushed his hat back from his face and gave one shake of his head. "Yes, I expect I do. I understand mighty well. My own pa fetched things over the mountains with him that he never found use for, but that still ain't gettin' this wagon through that sand, nor along the Arkansas bottom, either, where there's quicksand."

"When we come to a bridge, Mr. Vallian, we will cross it."

"Quicksand ain't no bridge, and as far as these sand-hills are concerned, you don't have to wait. They are here right now. All you got to do is roll on ahead."

He turned his horse. "And don't use yourself up. One night soon you'll have visitors."

"You mean that bunch from back there? You think they'd follow this far?"

"I think they have follered you. I think they are just a-settin' back waitin' for you to get bogged down or in some corner of the breaks where they'll have you dead to rights."

Duncan McKaskel let his hands fall to his sides. He knew his mules could not last much longer with the present load and the terrain he was crossing. He knew Susanna would be broken-hearted at leaving behind her possessions, and he did not want her to have to leave them behind. He knew the trail before them was long and bleak with only uncertainty beyond that. And now this.

He had been frightened that day in the town. He had gone ahead, and he remembered how each foot came down almost of its own volition as he moved forward. He had been walking ahead, moving into a trap with no thought of turning aside.

That had been in the open. Here there would be unseen enemies . . . and he remembered those men, a bad, bad lot.

"We will have to do the best we can," he said simply, "but now we have to be getting on."

He started the team, and they leaned into their harness, he took them gently, talking to them, urging them on. They started the wagon, and with the added strength of the sorrels, got through the first stretch of sand.

Night came before they cleared the sand-hills and got down to the bottom land near the river.

They camped where there was a good cool spring, with grass and water near Walnut Creek. As Duncan McKaskel stripped the harness from the horses and mules, he looked around for Con. He had disappeared.

"Did you see Mr. Vallian leave, Tom?"

"No, Pa. He was here one minute and when I looked around he was gone."

"We'll have a quick meal," McKaskel said, "and then we'll put out our fire."

When the boy started to gather sticks at a place near the wagon, McKaskel shook his head. "No . . . down in the hollow."

They wasted no time. Susanna made a quick pot of coffee and heated up some stew she had carried along in the wagon. When they had finished eating, the fire was put out and they moved back to the wagon.

Duncan had drawn the wagon among some trees and had the stock picketed nearby, but as darkness closed down he watered the stock again and brought them in close.

"Tom, you take the first watch," Duncan handed his gold watch to the boy. "When it's ten o'clock, you waken your mother."

Susanna slept in the wagon with the shotgun close by. She lay awake for a few minutes, regretting the red glow of the coals and worried by the rising wind.

Chapter VIII

H e came into the camp so softly she had no idea he was there until he spoke. "They're out there, ma'am. You'd better wake your man."

She had been sitting with her back against the wheel, the shotgun in her lap, and she had heard no sound nor movement but the wind in the trees.

"You move very quietly," she said.

"I don't know what they're figurin' on, but you'd better be ready."

He saw her move toward the wagon, then slipped back into the brush. The wind was strong and rising. It was going to rain . . . maybe hail. Vallian glanced at the sky, but it was so dark he could see no detail of the clouds, just a solid blackness. Far-off he heard a rumble of thunder, and he wondered if they had ever experienced a prairie thunderstorm. If they had not, they were in for a shock.

He held his rifle ready and went down through the trees, easing down a steep bank by passing himself from tree to tree where he could not have walked without them. At the bottom, close against a tree trunk, he listened.

It was a good night for an attack, too much noise to hear clearly, and constant movement of trees and brush. They would come along the creek bottom . . . their own camp was on the river or near it, not three hundred yards off. There was small chance that anyone else was anywhere around, but in the night the sound of the shots, if there were any, would not carry any distance at all.

By the dim firelight, he could make them out. There were eight. Doc Shabbitt was there, of course, and the Booster. Boston Pangman, Ike, and Purdy Mantle. The man crouching at the fire was Dobbs and then big Red Hyle. Con Vallian studied him for a moment. He knew all about Hyle.

Brutal, ruthless, contemptuous, and cold, Red Hyle was an Irish-Finn, quick with his hands, unusually strong, and a man utterly without regard for anyone. Red would be the worst of them. Purdy was good. Fast with his hands and a dead shot, but Purdy had a streak of decency in him, although how it ever got there was a question, and in that crowd it would be construed as weakness. He might hesitate to kill Hyle, but Hyle would not hesitate one instant to kill him . . . or anybody.

Nor would Doc Shabbitt, but Shabbitt was cautious. Doc would always try to have two aces in his pocket and another up his sleeve. He would kill and quickly, but only if your back was turned or he had a clean shot at a distance. Doc was officially the boss, but Con Vallian smiled cynically into the darkness. Doc could lead only as long as he could stay ahead of them, and he would much rather guide from behind.

They were taking their time. Suddenly he wondered —where was the Huron?

Vallian crouched, squatting at the foot of the tree, then he moved suddenly, swiftly, staying low. His body merged with that of a clump of brush.

The Huron!

He was out here . . . he had to be.

He had heard stories about the man. He was a skillful hunter, a stalker of game, and he had killed more than one man. He was like a ghost in the woods, and in this timber along the river, he was in his element.

Vallian strained his ears for sound, heard nothing. He straightened up, keeping himself merged with the brush, much of which was clumps of willow and some persimmon, and moved away. He was good, he told himself, but was he as good as the Huron? Was he even half as good?

He saw the shine of water from the river. On his right, between himself and the river the brush seemed to be an impenetrable wall. He crouched again, trying to identify the shapes around him.

Did something move? Or was it imagination? He eased his rifle forward in his hands.

The stab of flame struck his eyes before the report. The bullet was a whiplash in the night, then silence, but he did not move nor fire. If he moved now, he was a dead man.

The Huron had shot at what he believed was him, and waited for the return shot or the move . . . he did neither.

He knew the Huron was ready, the slightest move, the slightest sound and the second shot would have nailed him, so he held still, drawing slow, careful breaths and listening. Con Vallian knew that he might get only one shot and he wanted that one to do the job. If he missed . . . well, the Huron would not.

The night was very still. Along the stream there were a number of towering cottonwoods and many smaller trees with a dense stand of brush. Near the ground there were frequent gaps, and if a man could keep clear of the blackberry thickets with their thorns . . .

Vallian worked his way carefully, keeping close to

the ground, pausing to listen for any movement. The wind that had quieted for a time, now began to rise again, but it had shifted around. The lightning that had flared in the distance was nearer, there was a rumble of thunder, then a crash and a stab of lightning.

In that brief glare they saw each other, he and the Huron, and they were scarcely thirty yards apart. The Huron was luckier, for he was facing toward Vallian. Con turned sharply as he threw himself forward, landing on his shoulder and rolling into the turn. His gun came up, waiting for another lightning flash.

It came, and at the far side of the clearing the brush moved suddenly and Vallian broke a life-long habit. He shot at something he did not see. Instantly, from a dozen yards away, flame stabbed at him and he felt a sharp blow in his right side. He had started to rise, but the shot knocked him back into a sitting position. He fired instantly, then rolled swiftly away, feeling a stab of agony in his side.

He was hurt, badly hurt. Another bullet struck a few feet to his left, and he rolled over into a small hollow bedded with damp leaves. A shot went right over him, then another . . . searching fire.

Vallian rolled out of the hole and lunged to his feet. For a moment, clutching his rifle, he stood swaying . . . and then he moved away in the darkness. He was hit hard, in no shape to fight. His one thought now was to live . . . to exist, to get away.

His horse was some distance off, but he must have that horse.

The wagon? The McKaskels? No . . . too far away now, too hard to get to, and he'd be a trail to them.

The Indians. . . .

Susanna had not gone to bed. She waited, near the wagon, watching the night and Duncan.

He paced restlessly, worried. Suddenly they heard shots. She listened, hearing the sharp coughing reports, blunted toward the last by distance and the terrain.

"Duncan? Do you think they killed him?"

"Two of them were shooting . . . maybe three. I don't know."

Suddenly he knew what he had to do. He had a wife and son, and there was no time. He could not stay here to see if Con Vallian was alive or dead. The man was more fitted for this life than he, and there was no way in which he could help. The thing to do now was to insure the safety of his family.

"Susanna? Wake Tom up. We're going to leave."

She did not waste time. Duncan had hesitated, been uncertain, but now he spoke quickly, decisively. She shook Tom who was instantly awake. By the time they were out of the wagon Duncan had led up the horses. Tom took one side, he the other, and they threw on the harness, hooked up the traces.

In a matter of minutes they were rolling. "Where?" Susanna whispered.

He pointed with his whip-stock. "There . . . to the northwest. Away from the river."

They would not expect that. On the other hand, by day they would be out on the open plain, exposed for all to see. Nonetheless, she said nothing. They all rode and the mules moved out quickly, seemingly willing enough to turn their backs on the river. Maybe the shooting had made them uneasy.

He glanced at the stars, wishing he could tell time by them as some could. It must be an hour short of midnight . . . perhaps less than that.

The wagon made little enough sound in the wind and the rain and the first stretch was down a long slope to the west. The climb was harder, steeper, and the trail was muddy. Several times the mules made hard going of it but soon they were up and then they started out across the flat plains.

The wind whipped at their wagon-cover and the rain beat against it. In the occasional lightning flashes, they looked back, but they could see nothing, only distant, tossing trees, black against the suddenly gray grass when lightning flared and died.

The rain was making it harder for the mules. She

could feel the stronger pull they exerted, could see them leaning into the harness, and suddenly she was swept by guilt.

What a fool she was! To measure her husband's life and her son's life against these few things! They must be rid of them. Yet she waited. Now was not the time.

Guardedly, McKaskel looked at his watch. "I figure we're two miles off, Susanna. It isn't much . . . an hour's time, I'd say, and time is the thing."

They drove on, still heading northwest. After another hour they drew up to rest the mules. The rain was still falling, the wind blowing.

"I hope Vallian's all right," Susanna said.

"He will be."

"But he's all alone! He might be hurt!"

"He'll find us. We can do him no good if we're dead, or our stock gone. We've got to keep going."

When McKaskel saw the first gray of dawn he began searching for a place to hide. The land was no longer flat, it was gently rolling with a few ravines. Had the rain wiped out their trail? For awhile there it had rained hard enough, he was sure of that. If so, they might have lost their enemies, and Vallian, too.

He was almost glad of that. He hunched his shoulders against the rain and wondered if he had been jealous. No, he was sure of Susanna, and she was of him.

Of what was he jealous then? Of how awkward and helpless he must appear in the face of the other man's easy, deft movements? Con Vallian always knew just what to do, and he did not. He must appear a poor second to his wife and son.

It did not matter that back east, among their friends, Con Vallian would be considered an ignorant rustic. Out here was where they were, not back east.

Women were nothing if not realistic. They were practical. Their very nature as bearers of children made them so. For whenever they looked at a man there must always be the subconscious question of whether that man could take care of her and her children?

Well, he would have to learn. Maybe this was a wild goose chase, tearing off into the night like this without a trail, going God only knew where. Maybe he was stupid, but he had done it himself, he had made a decision and Susanna and Tom had jumped to help him.

I've learned something, he told himself. I've learned that it is better to move than just to sit. One has to act.

There was a dark fringe of something ahead and to the right. Only a glimpse, but it was there. He eased the team a bit further that way and after a few minutes he saw it, a hollow with a little timber. He drove along the edge, looking for a way down. He found a long slope, went down into it and pulled up near some trees.

"Tom? Get up on the hill, keep out of sight, and keep your eyes open.

"Susanna, we'd better have something to eat. I'll let the team have water and some time to graze."

It was only four or five acres of timber and brush, a small, hidden place with a spring and a trickle of water that ran off to the northeast.

"What are we doing, Duncan?" Susanna asked.

"With luck, we will rest out the day, and start again after sundown. We can't move very fast, so we will have to move at night, hide by day."

"But what about tracks?"

"I think the rain would wash out the first few miles of them. Some of that was pretty rocky, anyway. We've got a chance, and that's all."

They ate, took turns sleeping and watching. The horses drank, rolled, grazed, then drank again and rested. From a rocky, barren knoll featured only by some clumps of prickly pear, they watched the desert. In the distance they saw antelope. Tom knew he could trust the antelope to warn them, at least in that direction.

Rain fell softly through the day and the antelope disappeared. Once, far off, Tom thought he saw something moving, but he had only a glimpse, then nothing more.

Restless with lack of movement, Susanna walked down through the trees. They had stopped, found what was needed, and had gone no further, but now she walked into the deeper recesses of the woods, the area where the small ravine narrowed to a mere dimple in the hillside from the lower lip of which fell the water of the spring.

It fell upon sand and vanished to appear thirty or forty feet further along, and then to become a trickle three or four inches wide down to where the wagon was, and the horses.

Then she came upon a place where the rock had broken off and fallen, leaving a hollow overhang, a place such as cliff-dwellers used to wall up for houses. There was a shelter, five to seven feet high, twelve to fifteen feet deep at its deepest, and masked by brush. No rain penetrated here, not even with a strong wind from the west, because of the brush.

She walked back to camp. "Duncan? Could you and Tom and I carry that chiffonier? And the bed?"

"We loaded it, didn't we? I mean with your father's help. Yes, we could. Why?"

"Call him down and let's do it. Our wagon's too heavy, Duncan. Mr. Vallian was right."

Chapter IX

When the Huron walked into camp they all turned to look. He crossed to the fire and squatted there, taking up the coffee-pot, blackened from many fires, to fill his cup.

He was a tall, taciturn man in a buckskin shirt, homespun pants, and a battered black wool hat.

"Well? What happened?" Booster demanded.

The Huron sipped his coffee. "Good man," he said shortly, "very good man."

"Did you get him?"

"Maybe." The Huron sipped coffee then shrugged. "Maybe not. In the morning we will see."

"You didn't trace him down? You mean maybe he's lyin' out there?"

The Huron ignored the comment until he had eaten a strip of jerky, and then he said, "One does not go into the bush after a grizzly."

"I'll be damned," Shabbitt took his cigar from his teeth and regarded it, then brushed the ash away. "I don't understand you, Huron. Sometimes I think you're less an Injun than a white man, and an eddicated one to boot."

The Huron offered nothing, merely sipping his coffee. Finally he straightened up, rinsed his cup and walked to his bed.

As he lay down he stopped, just before stretching out. "He is a good man. If he is not dead, somebody will die."

"Come daylight," Ike Mantle said, "I'll have a look around. If he ain't dead, he better be."

Con Vallian had been hit hard and he knew it. Near the base of a tree he pulled moss from the tree and packed his wound. The bullet had gone through his thigh, but no bones were broken. After a moment's rest, he pulled himself up by clinging to brush and with a staff made from a broken branch, his rifle clutched in his left hand, he started on.

He made a hundred yards or so before he had to stop. He leaned against the bole of a tree, resting, panting heavily. By daylight there would be wolves on the scent, and he had to have left some blood sign back there. They would find that, then come after him.

Finding a small stream, rushing knee-deep after the rain, he stepped in and worked his way up stream. It would fool nobody, certainly not the Huron, but it might slow them down. He knew that a tracked man will usually come out of a stream on the same side he went in, but he went out on the opposite side, pulling himself up where the rocks were waist high.

For a few minutes he sat there in the rain, then with rifle and staff, pushed himself to his feet. He stood there, wavering from weakness, trying to make out his surroundings. A wink of firelight caught his eye . . . it was several hundred yards off, no doubt the camp of the Shabbitt outfit.

He made a dozen wobbling steps on the rock ledge before he had to step off, found another bare rock and managed to get to it. There was a long log going the way he wished to go, but he shied away. When it was wet like this the bark might slip off in places and that was the sort of sign the Huron could read at a dead-run.

He staggered on, hitching himself along. Twice he fell. Once he crawled for several hundred yards, then managed to get up again. When he got to where his horse had been, it was gone.

Even in the darkness he could see the white end of the broken branch. Frightened by something, a lion or wolf, probably, the horse had broken free and run off.

He wasted no time in cursing his luck, for that never helped. He did pause long enough to think the situation through, for much depended on what happened next.

They would not know his horse had run off. They would find its tracks and his and would conclude that he had mounted the horse and ridden away. Clinging to the bush he pulled off his boots, cut a rawhide string from the fringe of his jacket and tied them together by the loops and slung them over his shoulder.

He walked on. What to do? It would do no good to go to the McKaskels, and their wagon was far away now, at least a mile and in the wrong direction.

His first idea had been the best. He would go to the Indians. He had a rough idea of where their camp might be, and he started for it.

What followed was nightmare. He hadn't gone fifty steps when he tripped and tumbled into a ravine, losing his staff, but clinging to his rifle. How long he lay there he didn't know nor even when he started out again.

Somewhere along the way he became delirious. The loss of blood had weakened him, and he must have had a mounting fever. Perhaps it was only exhaustion, but all that followed was a hazy time of stumbling, staggering, moving—of falling, lying in the wet grass, rising and driving on. He went through trees and brush, tumbled into another gully and got himself out by crawling.

The moss came loose from the wound so he used grass.

He remembered lying on the grass and feeling hot sun on his back. Then he remembered trying to get up and hands taking hold of him. Somebody tried to take his rifle away and he clung to it. They tried to remove his gun belt and he struck the hands away and went to his knees, and then for a long time he remembered nothing at all.

It was a sensation of smothering and of wracking movement that awakened him. Suddenly he was awake, lucid, listening. He was moving, his body lay on an incline and he was wrapped in something coarse and smelly. His fingers touched his gun-belt. He still had it. A slight movement of his head and his cheek touched the cold of his rifle barrel.

He was lying on a travois wrapped in the folds of the buffalo-hide teepee. He was with the Indians then, and he was being moved. For some reason they were keeping him hidden.

Suddenly the horse that was pulling him stopped with a jerk, twisted a little, then was still. There was a confused sound of movement, the galloping of horses. Then a hoarse voice . . . Ike Mantle's voice. "You Injuns seen a wounded white man? We're huntin' him!"

"No see."

"You better not be lyin' to me, you Injun son-of-a—!"

"Ike! Shut up, damn you! That big buck yonder's got his rifle right across his saddle at you! *Lay off!*"

"Why? There's only six of them and they—"

"Eight," the Huron said calmly. "There are two others somewhere."

There was a moment of silence. "We're huntin' a bad white man," Doc Shabbitt said, "you Injuns find him, kill him or bring him to us, you savvy?"

Nobody said anything.

"I'd like to shake 'em down," Ike said angrily. "What's in all those bundles? What's on the travois?"

"Their lodges, Ike," Purdy said, "just the duffle they have to live with. Hell, if you want that gent so bad, let's hunt him. No use to start a war with these Injuns. We might whop 'em but we'd lose two or three and one of them might be you or me."

Red Hyle swung his horse away. "Let's ride!" he said roughly. "We don't care about him, anyway. Let's find that woman."

"All you think about's that woman," Booster said.

Vallian heard the sudden creak of a saddle, the movement of a turning horse. "What I think about's my own damn business. You want to make something of it?"

"Aw, Red! I was only makin' a joke! Forget it."

"What I want to know," Dobbs said suddenly, "is what's become of Boston? It ain't like him to ride off with no reason."

"He prob'ly thought he could find that gent," Booster said. "He saddled up early an' lit out. Said he had him a hunch.

"Somebody shot . . . just before daybreak it was. Somebody fired a shot off to the north."

"I heard no shot," Shabbitt said irritably. "If there was one it might have been them Injuns."

Con Vallian held himself very still, listening as the sound of the voices dwindled away with the sound of the horses' hoofs.

Boston Pangman gone and a shot fired . . . he scowled, puzzling over a vague recollection of something . . . he drew his pistol, barely able to get it from the holster within the confines of the buffalo hide teepee. He swung out the cylinder. Two chambers were empty . . . and he always reloaded.

He succeeded in getting the pistol back into its holster and slowly relaxed. They were moving again, moving on.

That night they unrolled him from his hide cocoon and bedded him down under some brush near their camp. There they brought him some broth made of venison, and one of the Indian women examined his wound and bathed it in some solution. The warm water felt soothing, and he could feel the warmth penetrating the sore muscles around the wound. She then wrapped the leg in a poultice, and left him alone.

He could lie there in the darkness watching the movement around the camp fire, but nobody came near him again or seemed aware of his existence. He understood that. They suspected they were being watched, and wanted Shabbitt and his men to see nothing that would lead them to suspect his presence.

When it was almost midnight a woman came to him with another cup of broth, then some coffee, almost too sweet with sugar. She sat by him while he ate, and once she put a hand on his brow, but she did not talk and shook her head when he started to speak. Before daybreak he was again rolled in the hide and tied to the travois.

He slept the day through. Twice a woman stopped near him, holding a bottle of water at her side, and he managed to take hold of it and drink. Again at night he was hidden and cared for.

On the third night, lying alone in the brush, he heard a faint stirring near the camp. His hand rested on his gun, and he listened again. Something was drawing near, moving very quietly. He heard a faint sound of metal striking a branch, a hoof-fall. Somebody was riding toward the camp, riding in the darkness.

He listened, straining his ears. The Indians appeared to be sleeping, the dogs made no sound. He drew his gun.

The movements drew nearer. He was still in no shape for a fight, although he seemed to be regaining his strength, but he did not want to fire a shot unless there was no alternative.

He eased back under his blankets, ears straining for

sound, his eyes upon the darkness. He must not shoot
. . . not until he knew what he faced.

The movements ceased. Firelight flickered on the
branches overhead. Suppose they simply fired into him
without appearing in the open where he could see
them? Suppose they gave him no chance?

Movement started then stopped again. Was the mysterious rider looking into camp? Was he close enough
for that? Why weren't the Indians awake? Why weren't
the dogs barking?

He turned his head and looked toward camp. All
was still. The coals glowed and a tendril of flame
burned some unconsumed branch on the far side of
the fire.

He thought suddenly of the McKaskels . . . where
were they?

The horse moved again, nearer.

He lifted himself to one elbow, the pistol in his
hand. He moved back the blanket and pulled himself
against the trunk of a small tree, waiting.

The steps drew nearer. The horse blew slightly
through its nostrils, and suddenly he had a hunch.
Catching a limb of the small tree he pulled himself
erect, balancing on his one good leg.

Holding his gun ready he made a small chirping
noise with his pursed lips.

There was silence, and he could picture the horse
standing, its ears up. And its rider?

The horse moved forward, pushed through the
brush, and suddenly an Indian, rifle in hand, was beside him.

The horse appeared, head up, ears up, nostrils dis-
tended.

"It's all right, boy," Con spoke softly. "It's all right.
It's me."

It was his own horse. Somehow, through the night
and the day and the miles, his horse had found him.
The horse came up to him, and Con put his hand
on its neck. He tied the horse to a branch near his

bed. The Indian disappeared in the brush on the far side of the fire. Con got back into his bed and pulled the blanket over him. He looked up at the horse. "It's all right," he said, "you're home again." And then he added, "as much of a home as we're likely to get."

Chapter X

For several days the wagon moved westward, and they saw no human being, nor sign of any. They had left off to the south the trail to Sante Fe and the westward lands, while the Overland Trail was far away over the northern horizon.

The rains had left water in buffalo wallows and holes beside the route they followed. At night they pointed their wagon-tongue westward, using the North Star as a guide, and by day the sun. The way they had taken was one no wagon had followed for it was far from water-holes and they were risking much in the days ahead.

They were quiet days. The wagon, relieved of much of its load, moved easily over the prairie grass. On the third day McKaskel killed a buffalo calf and, a few days later, a deer that he saw among the reeds near a small slough.

Each day the horizon was empty, they saw nothing, heard nothing, yet when a week had passed the water grew less, and Duncan grew worried. "We may have to turn south," he said, "I think we're running out of water."

"Let's try it another day," Susanna pleaded.

That day they saw a band of wild horses . . . hundreds of them who ran off a short distance and then stood, heads up, nostrils flared, looking toward them.

"I wonder what happened to him?" Susanna said suddenly. "Ever since the shooting that night, I've been worried."

McKaskel nodded. "So have I. And I've wondered if we shouldn't have stayed and waited for him."

"He said nothing about coming back," Susanna said. "He was a strange man."

That afternoon, only a few miles from their nooning, they came suddenly upon a small creek. They saw the tops of the cottonwoods first, then the fold in the plain where the creek ran.

"It's early," Susanna said, "but let's stop."

They found a flat just back from the creek among scattered cottonwoods, some of them huge old trees six or eight feet in diameter. There was much brush, and firewood enough for an army. They built a small fire, broiled some of the buffalo meat, and Tom caught a half dozen fish in the space of twenty minutes. If the stream had ever been fished, it must have been a long, long time ago. The water was clear, cold, and pure.

"I don't know what streams are in this area," McKaskel said. "I've no idea what this is. We should be west of Sand Creek, and we thought that was it we crossed some days back . . . it was running mighty shallow."

"It's water. Let us be thankful."

They gathered wood and stowed it in the tarp. They emptied both barrels of the remains of the water they had carried and refilled them with fresh water.

That evening, just before sundown, Duncan McKaskel killed another deer.

"I'll never forget this place, Duncan. It has brought us so much, water, wood, and fresh meat."

"Where's Tom?"

"Down by the creek. He was making a sailboat out of an old tin can and some sticks."

They sat still together, watching the slow finger of their smoke, lifting toward the sky. "This would be a good place, Susanna," McKaskel said, glancing around. "It has all we need. I think that flat-land up there would grow wheat."

"I want the mountains, Duncan. You promised me mountains."

He chuckled. "And you shall have them! We will start at daybreak."

Later that day they saw more wild horses and when they started in the morning the air was clear. Duncan pointed with his whip. "Susanna? Tom! The mountains!"

They were there, low on the horizon and faintly purple with distance.

He stared at them, thinking back. He had been, and was still, a greenhorn . . . a tenderfoot. There had been so much they did not know, and even the difficulties they had imagined were so much worse than expected. He had not expected the trouble when the shooting occurred, nor the vindictiveness of the men from that shabby little settlement.

Were they still following?

It was scarcely likely. They had seen nobody now for days, and the heavy rains must have washed out their tracks when first they moved away. Their wagon now was lighter by a good bit and did not leave the deeply cut tracks they would be hunting. He felt better, much better.

The mules moved out at a good gait, and Tom was singing in the back of the wagon. It was good to be alive. Beside him Susanna sat tall, looking toward the mountains.

Doc Shabbitt lit his cigar. "Santy Fee," he said, "there'll be good pickins at Santy Fee."

"What about the gold strike at Cherry Creek?" Hyle demanded. "Folks say they struck it rich!"

"I'll go anywheres," Booster McCutcheon said. "If'n we can't make out one way, we'll do it another."

"They got gold," Ike Mantle insisted. "I know they had gold in that wagon!"

"Beats me," Doc said, "what could have become of them. And that other gent, Huron, the one you had the fight with. What's become of him?"

"Well, we lost that wagon," Dobbs said, "looks like Red missed out on his woman."

"We haven't lost them," Purdy said, "but I say we're foolish to chase after a wagon-load of women's fixins and cabin furniture."

"What d' you mean . . . we haven't lost 'em?" Doc asked.

Purdy held up a tin boat made out of the top of a tin can, carefully bent into shape with a small stick for a thwart and another for a mast. "I found this down at the crick. Ain't rusted even a mite. I'd say some youngster made it, lost it playin' in the crick, an' she just floated down stream."

"Yeah," Doc studied it. "Surely ain't been in the water long. I'd say only a few miles."

"If we was to angle for northwest," Dobbs suggested, "we'd surely cut their sign."

Red Hyle got to his feet and walked to his saddle. Without a word he began to saddle up.

"Maybe Purdy's right," Booster said, "what if they ain't got nothin'?"

"The mules will be worth it at Cherry Creek. Where there's mines there's a market for mules."

Yet the trail was older than they believed. They found it, west of the creek by some distance, and the Huron rode up and down, studying the lay of the grass.

"This ain't the same," Booster said, "look at the tracks. The wagon we're lookin' for made deep tracks. She really cut deep!"

"Same wagon," the Huron said mildly. "Not so heavy now."

"What's that mean?" Shabbitt demanded.

"They have lightened their load," Purdy Mantle said quietly, "so they could travel faster."

"You mean they done buried the gold?" Ike said. "They wouldn't do a fool thing like that! Not way the hell an' gone out here!"

"I don't know anything about gold. That's just something we conjured up in our minds our own selves. I seen furniture all along the trail. They carry it a ways, then their stocks gets played out and they drop it. There's never been any gold."

"You say!" Ike sneered.

"Why go to the gold fields if you've already got gold? And why take gold to the gold fields?" Purdy asked.

"They got it," Ike insisted. "Anyway, they've got horses and mules and a wagon load of stuff."

"You seen many of those wagons, Ike?" Purdy asked gently. "Most of what they hold is important to nobody but them, except for tools, grub, and such. I never seen anything in a wagon yet that was worth the trouble to carry off."

"They can't be far," Dobbs said, "and we're goin' that way. Anyway, Red wants his woman."

"That's just a notion," Purdy said.

Red turned a little in the saddle. "It's my notion," Red said quietly, "and I like it."

Their eyes held for an instant and then Purdy shrugged and smiled. "Have at it," he said, "ever'body's entitled to a notion now and again."

He was smiling, but his eyes were still and watchful. Red turned abruptly away. "Let's get on," he said harshly. "Time's a-wastin'."

When morning came again there was a cool fresh wind coming down through the spruce, the aspen, and the pine trees. The wind had the smell of pines on its breath, and the sound of the aspen leaves stirring, and cool water over stones.

A dim road led off the bench down through the aspens and the cottonwood and almost without thinking, Duncan turned the mules down the faint tracks and they braked the wagon into the river bottom. Free of the trees, with marmots disappearing on every hand, there was a long green meadow, an old corral in the distance, and a faint track, overgrown with grass.

They were sitting tall on the wagon-seats now, and Tom had left his post at the rear to look at what they were approaching.

On the left were the aspens, their white trunks like the columns of a mosque, their leaves restlessly moving, always moving. The corral they were drawing near to was empty, the bars down, the grass within grown tall. The road dipped away to their right and they saw sunlight gleam on rushing water.

The gray of stones, a small field of them over which water had run and would run again, and then the stream, only a few feet wide at this point, but clear and maybe a couple of feet deep. Beyond the stream there was more forest and then the mountain, rising boldly up, bald and green at its higher points, the lower slopes thick with forest.

"Pa . . . look!"

Duncan McKaskel drew up. Beond the stream, not more than fifty or sixty yards beyond, was a cabin. It was a log cabin, patched with some cut boards, and it was old, obviously abandoned.

"Duncan. . . ? I love it."

"Let's look around."

He spoke to the mules and they moved ahead, ears pricked. "They like it too," he told himself.

They bumped and rumbled, splashing through the stream, struggled a little at the opposite bank because in the years between the river had cut it away somewhat, and then they were there.

The grass was green around the old cabin, the trees had been cleared back, behind it there was, some distance back, an old beaver pond with much gray, fallen timber, the bare ribs of a small and vanished forest. As he looked a fish plopped in one of the ponds, and ripples spread out.

He tied the reins and got stiffly down, stretching his back after the long sitting. Then he put up a hand and helped Susanna down.

Tom was already on the ground and running toward the cabin. He leaned into the open door. "Ma! It's got a floor!"

Susanna paused and looked all around. She listened to the gentle sound of the running water, the faint rustle of aspen leaves, the cloud shadows on the green dome of the mountain.

"Duncan? It is lovely, isn't it?"

"Yes . . . yes, it is. There's plenty of water, and there's grass."

The cabin was small, and it needed work, but it was the sound of running water and the aspen as well as the beaver ponds that made them like it.

"Duncan? Can we—?"

"We'll give it a try, Susanna. We'll stop for a few days while I look around." In his own mind, he was sure. He wanted to look at the higher ground first though.

There was room enough for a kitchen garden, and perhaps a crop of corn and potatoes . . . some beans.

Duncan McKaskel walked back to the wagon and began to unhitch. There were things to be seen, he must look around, but in his own mind this was home.

Whoever had built the cabin had abandoned it long ago. Judging by the look of the logs and the weathering, he would guess ten years or more. Nor was there any sign of occupancy of even the casual sort. By leaving the known trails, the prescribed route, they had come to this place, come as if guided by fate.

Picketing the horses and mules on the rich green grass, after watering them, he began to gather firewood, and as in any forest, it was scattered everywhere. Much heavy stuff had been washed down by the stream, and there were dead-falls and many trees killed by beavers. There was wood enough to last a winter through.

"We will sleep in our camp tonight," he suggested, "and tomorrow we'll clean up the house and repair what is needed."

Leaving Tom to gather more wood and Susanna to prepare supper, he took his rifle and walked up the dim game trail toward the bench above the river-bottom.

It was broad and green, sweeping away, several hundred acres of excellent pasture, toward the aspens at the foot of the mountain. He saw the tracks and droppings of both deer and elk, and the track of a bear.

He stood still, drinking in the quiet beauty of the place. Suddenly, among the aspens beyond the meadow he saw something move, and a moment later it moved forward just a little, pausing in a spot of sunlight.

A bull elk, and a big one.

He started to lift his rifle, then hesitated, not wishing to shatter the stillness with a rifle shot. He smiled at himself, then lowered the rifle and turned away. They had meat enough for now, and if he knew Tom he would be fishing before noon tomorrow.

Carrying his rifle in the hollow of his arm, he walked back down the trail to the cabin. Tom had kindled a camp fire, and the smoke was rising slowly.

They had come a long way, but it was worth it. The shadows grew longer, and for a moment he stood half-way down the trail, looking at all that lay below. It was a quiet place, a lovely place, but suddenly he felt a shudder of fear.

They were alone, so very alone!

How far away was Cherry Creek? Were there nearer settlements? Or any neighbors at all? Suppose he should be injured? Unable to work?

Their food supplies were very low, and must be augmented by hunting and fishing. Tom was a good fisherman, and was on the way toward becoming a hunter, but that was not enough. They must plant their seed, once they had ploughed and harrowed the ground, and they must jerk some meat, and in the meanwhile, scout a little further around to see what trails there were, what neighbors they had.

This was, he believed, the land of the Ute, and the Utes were a fearless and warlike people, yet they had often been friendly to the white man.

He walked down to the fire. "Susanna, the first thing tomorrow, measure your flour, salt, coffee, sugar, and bacon. We'll have to see just where we stand.

"There's plenty of game." He hesitated, a little embarrassed. "I saw an elk up there. I just couldn't shoot him."

"Let's not hunt close by, Duncan. We don't have to, do we?"

"It would be better not to," he said thoughtfully. "If anything goes wrong we may not want to go too far afield for meat."

She looked at him quickly. She knew him very well indeed, and she felt the sudden change in mood.

"Is something wrong? Doesn't the place look right?"

"No, it's fine. It has everything. Everything but neighbors, I am afraid."

"You think they are following us, don't you?"

He hesitated before replying, but he had never been one who believed women should be sheltered. Protected, cared for, but not kept in ignorance. "Yes, I do. We have to think that way, Susanna, and if we are wrong we will have lost nothing."

He squatted and fed some sticks into the fire. And in the moment of stillness after their talking stopped, they both heard it. A single shot.

Chapter XI

For a moment, neither moved. He squatted on his heels, she standing beside the fire, coffee-pot in hand. A shot?

Well, why not? They were not alone in the world, no matter how much it seemed so. There were sure to be prospectors, hunters, trappers, Indians. . . .

"Maybe we do have neighbors," he said striving to keep his tone casual.

How far would the sound of a shot carry? In this clear air, perhaps as much as a mile, or even further. Yet whoever fired that shot was not far off, certainly within two miles. And that would imply they might have a neighbor.

Or that the Doc Shabbitt outfit had caught up with them.

"Somebody hunting meat," Duncan added. "Only one shot . . . and at this hour. I'd say somebody killed a deer or an elk."

Tom caught three good-sized trout that evening, but

they kept their fire small, cooked and ate the trout fresh from the stream, and by daylight Duncan started to examine the house. While he checked it over to see what needed to be done, Susanna went through their supplies. Their gifts to the Indians had cut sharply into their small hoard.

Only a few pounds of flour remained, and only three cupfuls of sugar. There was a slab of bacon, some dried apples, and the condiments. Fortunately there was a good supply of coffee and several pounds of tea scarcely touched.

Duncan listened while she told him and nodded. "All right, we will have to take it easy. Tom's fish supplied our supper, and we've enough venison left for breakfast. Tomorrow I'll go hunting."

That day they cleaned and mopped the cabin, wiping down the ceiling and walls, cleaning the cobwebs from the corners of the loft. There had never been glass in the windows, just strips of canvas tied over them to let light in and keep the rain out. The cabin had two rooms, a bedroom and a combination living room and kitchen. There was a lean-to where wood had been stored.

"That's your job, Tom," Duncan told him. "You can fill it up."

Tom looked at it, appalled. "Pa! That'll take days!"

"It will take days, perhaps weeks, but if we stay here it must be filled. Keep a corner for kindling, pitch-pine, and fine stuff to start fires."

The following day, several miles to the south, Duncan killed a deer, skinned it out and brought the hide and the best cuts of meat back to the cabin, and Susanna found the first of the strawberries. They were small but of excellent flavor.

Yet the sound of that one shot disturbed them. Duncan McKaskel knew they would have no rest until it was discovered who had fired that shot, and why.

On the morning of the third day he saddled the blaze-faced sorrel with the three white stockings. "Stay close," he said, "and keep the shotgun at hand. I will be gone several hours, but will definitely be back before dark. If I see any game I'll try to bring back some meat."

They watched him ride away into the aspens. He rode toward the mountain, and upstream. Susanna knew he intended to circle around and study the country.

Susanna heated water and began to wash clothes. Tom went to picking up fallen limbs, chunks of fallen trees and odds and ends of bark for fuel.

As she looked about her, Susanna was concerned about all that must be done before cold weather came upon them, and once more she thought how ill-fitted they were for the life they had begun.

When she had finished her washing and hung the clothes out to dry on a string from the wagon to the corner of the cabin, she got a sheet of paper and began to list what was needed. Once snow fell there was little they could do to obtain supplies, so all must be had beforehand.

Always her ears listened for a shot, but she heard no sound. Tom walked out through the trees, and swung back to their trail. When he returned to the cabin he said, "There are no tracks. At least, none that I could see. The wind and the rain have wiped them out."

They could not be found then. They were safe. Yet even as she thought it she knew they must always be alert, always ready. The afternoon was warm, and restlessly, she walked down to the river. Tom had a line in the water but he shook his head when she started to speak.

She had started to turn away when some movement caught her eye and she looked up. A rider sat on the edge of the bluff just beyond the trees. He was no one with whom she was acquainted, nor did the horse seem familiar. He was looking at something to their north and she slowly eased back to the brush, motioning to Tom.

Tom drew his line in and slipped back beside her. Crouching together, they watched the man.

For some time he sat there without moving. Then he turned his horse and started down the trail into the river-bottom. As his face turned toward them, Susanna gasped.

The man's nose was flattened on his face, and even at this distance she seemed to see some discoloration on his face, yet it might only have been the shadows of leaves. He had almost reached the bottom of the short trail when he pulled up sharply, then swung his mount and rode back up the trail.

Far off they heard a faint call.

When he was gone they went quickly back to the cabin, and Tom looked to see if the shotgun was loaded. It was.

"It was that man, Tom, I am sure of it. It was the man I hit that night."

"He certainly had a bashed-in nose," Tom said. "Do you think he knows who did it?"

"One of us, certainly. Tom, I wish your father was back. I wonder how they found us?"

"I don't believe they have," Tom said, "or else he would not have turned around and gone off. They're just looking around."

She considered that. From where he had stopped the cabin was not in view, nor could their wagon have been seen. The horse and mules were in the pasture on the bench above the cabin.

"Tom," she said suddenly, "go get Amby and bring him down here, and the mules, too. We'll water them and keep them close to the house tonight."

"I've found a place back in the aspen that's just like a stable," he said, "there's shelter from the wind and some shelter from rain. It wouldn't take much to fix it up."

Fortunately, they had no fire. The water had been heated some time before and that fire had died down. Otherwise that man could have detected the smoke. She watched Tom trudge up the trail to the bench, and then she got the shotgun and went to the chest for extra shells. She put four in each pocket of her apron.

Where was Duncan? She had heard no shot, no sound since he had left, hours before. The shadows grew longer. Light bathed the summit of the bald mountain but there was no sound, nothing to disturb the cool evening.

Duncan had said he would be back before dark, and he was not yet back. She felt a strange tightness in her throat . . . was it fear? Her eyes turned to the trail from the bench.

Tom should be coming back. It was not as if the animals were running loose, they had been picketed, all of them. Nervously, she walked across the grass . . . listening.

An owl spoke mournfully from the cottonwoods near the river. Was it an owl? Didn't Indians sometimes call to each other that way?

She took up the shotgun and started toward the trail. Yet she had taken only a step when she heard a hoof strike stone and she stopped very still.

"Well, now. And all alone, too."

She turned. The shotgun was hidden in the folds of her skirt. She did not believe they had seen it. After a first chill of sheer panic, her nerves steadied.

The man with the flat nose and another one, a slender, dark man with a buckskin jacket stood before her.

"All alone," the man with the flat nose repeated, "we surely lucked out, didn't we, Huron?"

"I am not quite alone," Susanna said quietly, "but it does not matter, does it, *gentlemen?*"

Booster chuckled. "Flattery gets you nowhere, ma'am, nowhere at all. I ain't no gent an' never pretended that I was."

She stood very still and tall. Booster drew his foot from the stirrup. "Now, ma'am, we know you're all alone, and if you want to make trouble you can, but it just ain't goin' to do you no good."

"Will nothing influence you to just ride on? We just

want to build a home here. We wish trouble to no one."

Booster chuckled. "Now that's right nice of you, ma'am. I always like to come up with folks like you, who don't want trouble, because it saves a heap of sweat."

"If nothing else will influence you," Susanna lifted the shotgun waist-high, "how about this?"

Even as she said it she was surprised that she, Susanna McKaskel could say such a thing, but her hands were steady as she held the shotgun. Con Vallian, she thought, would have been proud of her.

Booster stopped. "Now, ma'am, you be careful. That thing might be loaded."

"It is," she replied quietly, "and my husband tells me this will be very destructive at this range. I will hope I do not have to find out . . . I do not like the sight of blood, gentlemen."

Booster stared at her. He was angry but he was also scared. Would she shoot? She sounded very cool, and although she might be too frightened to shoot, he was not at all sure he wanted to make the test. A shotgun, at that range, could rip a man in two.

"Now, ma'am—"

The Huron spoke for the first time. "Booster, you are becoming a little hasty. Have you thought what Red would say to this?"

For the moment Booster had . . . and he knew very well what Red Hyle would say. "You've got a point there, Huron," he said, "maybe we should just ride back to camp."

Suddenly there was a faint rattle of stones from the bench trail. Both men turned sharply, and when they did, Susanna, moved over behind them. "Go now . . . and don't come back."

Booster McCutcheon looked around. "Oh we'll go!" he said, "but we'll be back, too. We got a man who is mighty wishful of knowin' you, ma'am, and when we come back we'll all come."

The Huron had turned his horse back toward the

river and was walking it away. Booster, glad of an excuse to leave Susanna and the shotgun behind, turned and followed. A shotgun, especially in the hands of a scared woman, was a dangerous thing.

Susanna turned and walked back toward the cabin, then stood there, listening to the retreating sound of their horses' hoofs. She heard them splash through the river and heard the click of hoofs on stone as they crossed the wide bed of rocks that covered part of the stream bed.

Then she heard Tom coming, with their own stock. "Ma? Are they gone?"

"Yes, I think they are . . . for the time being."

"Boy, Ma, you were terrific! I was scared, really scared!"

"So was I."

"You sure didn't act scared. Wow! The way you threw down on them—!"

" 'Threw down'! Tom, what kind of talk is that?"

"Well, anyway, you sure made them back up. Wait until I tell Pa—"

"He should be home soon. Let's go inside and light a lamp, and you can build up a fire. They know where we are now, but I doubt if they will come back this night. In any event, we shall be ready for them.

"Your father will be tired and we must have some coffee ready for him, and a hot meal."

She tried to make her voice sound confident, but she was frightened. What if something had happened? What if some of the others had found Duncan and there had been trouble? Still, there had been no shooting . . . but suppose they were in some canyon? Could she still have heard?

Susanna lighted the lamp, then replaced the chimney. She glanced at the doorway, and realized that the light within made the darkness without even more intense. Leaving the lamp on the mantel she went outside where Tom was kindling the camp fire.

She looked again toward the darkness of the forest,

and the silver of the water. The gravel bench at the water's edge looked white now.

Where was Duncan?

"Ma? Don't worry. There's lots of reasons why he might not make it on time. He may be across the river and it's very deep in some places. Maybe he's looking for a place to cross, or has to ride around some thick brush. And sometimes somebody stays out longer than they planned, without realizing."

What he said was true, of course, but Tom's reasoning did not allay her fears. Something was wrong, and she knew it.

"He's lying hurt somewhere, I just know it!"

"Aw, Ma—! He maybe couldn't find his way home in the dark and just stopped where he was. That would be the wisest thing. Con told me that if you figured you were lost the best thing was to stop right where you were until daylight, then think yourself out of it."

"I wish he was here now."

"We've got to do for ourselves, Ma. We can't always be trusting to him to come along and pull us out. I found a place, back in the aspens, where somebody had made a sort of hidden corral with dead aspen logs. Indians, maybe."

"What are you suggesting?"

"We could hide the mules. Three of them, anyway. We . . . me, I should say, I can ride old Balaam. You could take one of the sorrels."

"All right, Tom. When daylight comes if he is not here, we'll look for him. It's better than just waiting for them to come back."

Chapter XII

Con Vallian left the Indians on the tenth day. His leg was still stiff and needed careful handling, but once in the saddle he was ready to travel. He thanked the Indians, shook hands all around, and rode out to the westward.

Running Wolf squatted beside him at the fire on the morning he was to ride out. "You friend," he said, "he leaves somethings."

After some casual talk and a few questions, Con grinned. So they had begun to learn, after all. Well, maybe they would make it.

They had left, he gathered, some articles of furniture. The Indians, scouting around, had found indications and had looked further. Knowing these things had belonged to the friends of the man at their camp, they had left them alone.

The Indians, who were constantly on the move and missed very little gave him the direction of the Mc-Kaskels' wagon.

"Smart," he decided, "or lucky." They had left the

trails behind and had taken a high country route that normally could not be traveled for lack of water. Now, with the recent rains and pools in the buffalo wallows, they could make it through.

He lost their trail within a few hours due to rains and wind, so he took a long swing south, riding late in the evening and at night. On the second day after leaving the Indians he came up with the trail of the Shabbitt outfit. They were headed west, following the usual trail, but here and there they left sign enough to indicate they were doing a lot of scouting . . . scouting for the wagon trail McKaskel would leave.

He checked all their campsites with care. There were only seven of them now . . . he had his own vague recollection of a difficulty with Pangman. Somehow, when wandering and delirious, they had met.

Pangman's tracks were missing, and Vallian had two loads gone from his six-shooter. As bad off as he must have been, he had obviously been good enough.

At the fourth camp he checked, he found that they had camped by a stream. It was a small one, and even he had not been aware of its existence. He went over the camp with care, and his attention paid off.

He found some bloody rags first, probably a bandage Booster McCutcheon had used on his face. And then he found the tin boat, bent out of shape and cast aside. They had camped on the edge of a stream, and without doubt they had found the boat there, where it had floated down from above.

What followed next needed no guess work. When the Shabbitt outfit rode out they rode northwest.

Most of their riding had been done after the rains had passed and their trail could be followed even by night. He rode swiftly, only pausing to rest his mustang from time to time.

It was none of his affair in one sense, but in another it was. He had advised the McKaskels, helped them, eaten their bread and food, drunk their coffee. He was not a man to take such things lightly.

On the first day he rode thirty miles, on the second

he covered fifty. The Shabbitt outfit had a tough trail to find, and were probably riding by guess as much as by sight. He had no such problem. If he could find the Shabbitt bunch he would either find the McKaskels or he would discover what had happened to them.

Before him loomed the eastern wall of the mountains, cut by deep canyons, furrowed by lesser ravines, openings that gave on to lovely mountain meadows or to tumbling cataracts. They might have gone into any one of them.

Yet he knew that most people, traveling in the wilds, will follow the line of least resistance. This would be especially true of a man traveling with a wagon and a family. So Con Vallian took his time.

The change had been abrupt. From the short grass country he had suddenly ridden into a sub-alpine world where the grass was richer and the wild flowers everywhere. There were scattered stands of ponderosa and from time to time he drew up to scan the country ahead.

Any tracks would be washed out or damped down by subsequent rains, but to pass through a country and leave no mark of one's passing is nearly impossible. Peering from under the brim of his hat, he studied the lay of the grass, the possible ways a wagon might have taken.

They had made a mistake by coming in close to the mountains because if they wished to go to Cherry Creek they must follow along the mountains which meant crossing many gullies or canyons where the streams flowed from the higher country. Yet it was the mountains toward which they were bound, and it might be they would turn off.

He scanned the area thoughtfully, looking for some favorable opening into the back country. Then he started on, casting about for a lead. Under the aspens and close to their groves were stands of golden cinquefoil, and in the groves a bit further along, columbine. Often they were mixed with other flowers. The grass was wet from heavy dews or what was left of the recent rains.

He worked his way along the edge of the forest, riding in and out of the trees, weaving a careful way, alert for ambush and any sign of travel. He saw the fresh droppings of deer and elk, he saw where a bear had clawed high upon a tree . . . only hours ago, by the look of it, and once he found a lion kill, half-eaten and buried under brush.

Unconsciously he had worked his way higher upon the mountain, following the easiest route, yet aware that one can often see tracks from up high that would be missed on the ground and close by.

He was emerging from a stand of spruce when he caught a glimpse of movement . . . several riders, rifles in hand, moving along an open meadow at a lope.

"Shabbitt!" He swore softly. Even at the distance he could recognize several of them, and it was equally obvious that they were going somewhere, not just wandering or searching. Then, faintly, his eyes seemed to pick up the track of a wagon!

He stood up in the saddle and tried to see along the slope to his right. They were riding into a gap in the hills where the wagon, if those really were tracks and not his imagination, had gone. They rode as if expecting trouble.

Turning his mount, he rode swiftly along the mountain side in their direction, and cutting down through the trees, although keeping under cover, he came upon a game trail.

It was a chance, and he took it, knowing at the same time that many such trails can be useless for horses. A deer, holding its head low, can often go under limbs and brush that a horse must skirt around . . . and often enough the hillside is too steep for such travel.

Suddenly, ahead of him, he saw a thin trail of smoke. There was no way he could arrive before the Shabbitt outfit. No way at all.

They were closing in on the place below, riding up the stream . . . yet, looking at it from above he could see they must slow down, for soon there would be no good way to go unless they took to the water. Even then their progress would be slowed.

Far off to his left now he could see a dim trail that led up the canyon, and the place to which they seemed to be going lay due north from where he now was.

Here and there the growth thinned down and it was becoming more and more difficult to keep out of sight. He shucked his rifle, holding it ready in his hands. One man alone against seven, he must trust to surprise.

He dipped down through the trees, crossed a low saddle and down to a bench. Unknown to him he was coming in to the cabin from the east and was riding down to the bench where Duncan McKaskel had pastured his mules.

Emerging from the aspens, he drew up, listening. He had gotten a little ahead of them, for they had to skirt dead-falls and driftwood, and the footing along the rocky stream-bed was not good for fast riding.

He cantered across the pasture, skirting a small lake, and drew up among the trees near the edge of the bluff that dropped off into the wide river bottom. He heard no sound from below.

Weaving through the trees, ducking for the lowest branches, he pulled up suddenly. Below him were some old beaver ponds, with many fallen logs, some dead trees standing, and the smooth, clear water of the ponds. As he watched he could see the widening ripple where a beaver swam . . . unalarmed.

Turning his head he saw the cabins, and near them, the wagon. No horses or mules, no movement, no sign of life. Perhaps the merest shadow of smoke from the campfire near the wagon.

The beaver was working away, undisturbed.

He listened, and thought he detected a faint splashing. He glanced at the pond . . . the beaver was gone.

Several marmots were in sight, bustling brown bundles of fur, playing on the green grass below. One of them was within thirty feet of the house.

It was empty then.

Duncan McKaskel, his wife, and son were gone.

Where?

A faint sound reached him and he glanced downstream.

They were in sight now, riding through the scattered trees beyond the beaver ponds, partly shadowed by the cottonwoods, the narrow-leaved trees of the high country. They emerged on the far bank, and scattering out, picked their way across.

In a sudden rush, they swept up to the house and leaped from their saddles. Red Hyle was first at the door. He emerged at the rear door, glancing all around, swearing.

Ike Mantle had gone for the wagon. He could be heard moving around in the wagon, then he thrust his head out. "Hell, there's nothing here! Not a damn thing!"

Slowly they came out, looking all around. They were no more than sixty yards off and their voices carried easily in the clear air.

"Gone. Now where the hell—?" Dobbs was saying.

Of them all, only Purdy Mantle seemed undisturbed. "It wasn't worth the trouble," he said disgustedly. "I don't think they ever had anything, anyway."

"They left their wagon and their clothes an' stuff. They'll be back."

"Back when?" Shabbitt asked irritably. "Hell, maybe they just figured to Hell with it an' left their wagon an' all. If they had gold, they done taken it with them. To Cherry Creek, more'n likely."

"We can wait for 'em," Booster suggested, halfheartedly.

Ike Mantle was disgusted. "We've wasted enough time. "If we pick up their sign, we'll follow on. I think they got the gold with 'em, or it's buried. Maybe it's buried right here."

They stirred around, searching the house again, and

the wagon. Suddenly, Booster pointed. "Look! There's been some diggin', yonder!"

He indicated the corner of the yard some distance from the cabin where Duncan had begun spading up a garden.

"Hell, that's just a garden! He's figurin' on growin' corn or peas or something."

"Yeah? An' what better place to hide something? Right where nobody'd be surprised to see the ground dug up?"

Several of them started for it. Red Hyle looked on in disgust, then walked to his saddle horse and stood there, one hand on the pommel, the other on the cantle, his head bowed.

On the slope above, Con Vallian watched the men a moment longer. In a few minutes they would start hunting for sign. They would look around and try to find any tracks left by the McKaskels, so he knew he'd better get at it first.

He rode swiftly through the trees, changing direction a dozen times to find a way through, always reaching the same short, steep bluff. But this time among the trees, riding over the edge he let his horse slide to the bottom, then crossed deliberately toward the stream. He found a narrow trail, apparently leading from the cabins below to somewhere north. In the trail were the hoof-prints of several horses and at least one mule.

Crouching low to avoid overhanging limbs, he rode swiftly along the trail, crossing the stream over and back several times and suddenly emerging into a small clearing.

Obviously someone had worked a claim here. There was a rocker, long unused, and even a rusted shovel and pick. On the far side the trail led out of the clearing and away from the creek.

Pausing to listen, he heard no sound, but followed the trail up out of the river bottom as it turned sharply left and back to the southeast.

Now what was this? Returning the way he had come?

Not quite. He had reached the point of a triangle and was now taking a route back south, away from the steepest mountains, but much farther to the west.

Nobody had left the trail. Like him they were following a well-marked route. Yet now, out in the open and away from the shadows he noticed something he had missed . . . the trail of one of the horses was several hours older than the following horse and mule.

What did it mean?

Somebody had left the cabin, had not returned, and the others were following after. The first horse carried the heavier rider—Duncan McKaskel.

He rode into a small grassy hollow and started toward the other bank when he pulled up sharply, hearing voices. Slowly, he walked his horse on up.

Susanna and Tom were there, Susanna on one of the sorrels, Tom on a mule. In the clearing, not twenty feet from them stood the other sorrel. Its haunches were bloody, and its saddle turned under its belly.

There was no sign of Duncan McKaskel.

Chapter XIII

Con Vallian sat, taking in the scene. He knew better than to go charging into such a situation. Duncan McKaskel might be lying close by, his body hidden by grass or brush, and his attackers might be nearby, also waiting for those who would come after McKaskel.

Susanna was down on the ground, looking quickly about her. The boy went to the horse and began removing the saddle.

Staying near the edge of the trees, Vallian slowly rode in a half-circle toward the tableau before him. He held his rifle easy in his hands, prepared for whatever might come. Nothing in his life had prepared him for things to turn out right. When they did, he was pleased, when they did not, he was ready.

As he rode his eyes swept the earth for tracks. He was sure, since Susanna and Tom had obviously not found McKaskel, that Duncan had been hurt elsewhere. His frightened horse had run off, leaving him stranded and afoot. On the plains that could be the death of a man, in the mountains, where there was water and food, even if a man knew where to look, it could still mean trouble.

Before he reached them he found the trail. The sorrel had come plunging down a steep bank, dragging a whip of a broken branch along with it.

He glanced up the bank. The horse had still been frightened when it came over the bank, so it might not have come far.

He rode up to them and they turned swiftly. "Get that saddle cinched up," he said flatly, "and mount up. We're a-wastin' time."

"Mr. Vallian! My husband is hurt! He is somewhere around here and—"

"No, ma'am. He's nowhere around there. He's back yonder," Vallian jerked his head toward the east, "an' he may be hurt, but if we don't get out of here, we'll all be in a fix. That Shabbitt outfit found your place, and they'll be trailin' after."

Leading the sorrel, they turned and followed Vallian.

He was thinking fast. They would find that trail as easy as he had, and they'd come following after. No sense in going up that bank . . . he doubted if the woman and boy could make it, anyway, and he knew that atop the bank there was a long gap in the trees that led away toward the foot of a mountain.

Chances are the horse had come running right down that open space, and that he hadn't run more than a mile.

He had not taken the time to do more than glance at the horse. The scratches might be those of a lion, or perhaps it was only gouged by the forks of a broken branch. There was no time to stop and make sure, and it was unimportant in the long run. First they had to try to find McKaskel, and then they had to find a place to hole up. If they did not find McKaskel right away, the second would have to come first.

He turned in his saddle and glanced back. No dust in this country. The trails were seldom used and too grassy. There was a chance they might stop at the cabin and wait, but it was more likely they'd come on.

You got yourself in one hell of a mess, he told himself irritably. *Why can't you stay out of other folks' affairs? These people are nothing to you.*

Well, they weren't anything to him. Only that Susanna woman, she made a right good pot of coffee, and where was he going anyway? Besides, he liked to hear McKaskel talk. It wasn't every day a man encountered a real educated gentleman.

He led the way and he did not look back. The trail was one a blind man could follow, and there was no need to cast about. The gelding had come out of those woods like the mill-tails of Hell, bleeding some, too. He could see the bright crimson flecks of blood as he rode, and the trail through the tall grass was plain.

How long had McKaskel stayed with the gelding? Probably he'd been thrown right off. It looked like a lion had jumped the horse, maybe a young lion who didn't know any better, or one who saw the horse but not the man and sprang in hunger and haste. The horse would have leaped, fought, struggled, tumbling Duncan McKaskel into the brush. He might have been hurt seriously, simply scratched by brush, or attacked by the lion.

These western lands brought death suddenly, without warning, and in a hundred ways. It had a way of exploding into violent action leaving a man broken and bleeding, far from any help. Many a father or son rode away never to return, many a lone hunter left coffee on the fire to picket a horse or fetch a bucket of water, and that was the end of him. Sometimes his bones were found. Often enough not even that.

Con Vallian drew up, listening. The following horses stopped one by one, and in the silence he strained his ears beyond their breathing, beyond the little sounds of their presence, yet he heard nothing.

Sunlight fell through the trees, bringing a shattered radiance into the gloom, the aspens poised in slender beauty along the way, and the moss on the rocks was of the deepest green. Nearby, in a small, swift-running stream, a dipper sat on a rock, cocking its head toward some unseen life at the stream's bottom. The bird bobbed, disappeared into the foam at the base of a small waterfall, then came up suddenly.

His eyes searched the green-shadowed stillness, and then he touched the mustang with his heel and it moved on, walking with delicate feet upon the damp leaves in the trail.

Con was worried. He would have preferred a sound, something he could place and identify. Were they following or not? And where was McKaskel?

He was back-tracking the sorrel, finding a tiny fleck of blood here, a crushed leaf there, the indentation of a hoof's edge somewhere else. They had entered a narrowing ravine, thick with a stand of trees, some rocks, many dead-falls. Con hesitated, his eyes scanning the narrow spaces among the trees, but there were not many places from which the horse could have come.

What he saw was slight, a tendril of bark hanging from a rotting trunk, still damp where it had been knocked loose from its place. Further on he found where a hoof had slipped on some wet leaves, and worked his way upward, the others single file behind him.

They emerged into the sunlight. Running hoofs had left their tracks in the open there, on the west slope of the mountain. They followed, crossed over the shoulder, and almost at once they saw him.

Duncan McKaskel was drawn back against a tree, and his shirt was bloody, there was a cut on his head and blood matted his scalp.

"Thank God!" he said fervently. "How'd you find me?"

Susanna dropped to the ground and ran to him.

"There's no fresh blood," Vallian commented, "looks like it's stopped. We've got to get him off this slope and down into the canyon."

"You mean to move him? You can't!"

Con Vallian was pushing and prodding, looking McKaskel over thoroughly. "My guess would be you got you a badly bruised leg, a busted rib or two, and a cut on your scalp. You got a few scratches here and there but otherwise they don't amount to much.

"You'll be laid up for awhile, but you'll live." He grinned. "I reckon you will. I seen tenderfeet die of things wouldn't hurt a ten-year old girl out here, an' maybe you will, too.

"We got to get you off this rise. Be cold here tonight, mighty cold. Anybody huntin' you would have no trouble, out in the open like this."

"It was a lion," McKaskel said, "a lion jumped on my horse. My horse threw me but I managed to get a shot at it."

"Scared it," Vallian said. "Lucky you didn't hit it. A hurt mountain lion is a nasty piece of business, apt to cut up somethin' fierce."

"I think you are the most callous man I ever knew!" Susanna said hotly. "I don't think you're even sorry!"

"He ain't no kin to me, ma'am," Vallian replied, smiling, "an' out here in this country a man can get scratched up worse'n that doin' his day's work. I mind the time I had to amputate a finger."

Vallian reached down a hand. "Mac, you grab aholt. Have you in the saddle in no time."

"Now, see here!" Susanna protested.

"Ma'am, the sun will be down in an hour. Maybe less. When the sun goes down up here it'll be cold, cold like you never seen it. We're high-up . . . maybe ten thousand feet . . . so we'd better get down where we can build an' hide a fire and get out of the wind."

Duncan clasped his hand, and Vallian pulled him up and helped him on his horse. McKaskel's face was gray with pain, but aside from a grunt as he heaved into the saddle, he managed to make no sound.

Vallian grinned at him. "You got you a little sand there, man. You nourish it some and you're apt to turn out quite a westerner."

"It's easy to be brave when all you have to do is talk!" Susanna said sharply.

Vallian chuckled, and rode out ahead of them until he came to a place to make camp.

"Well, here we are, McKaskel. We'll camp right here. Plenty of cover, firewood, water, and rocks and logs to fort up in case they should find us."

Chapter XIV

Where they stopped there were aspens and an acre or two of meadow, thick with grass. An outcropping of boulders offered shelter, and there was dead wood enough to last for years, the result of some long ago blow-down when a fierce wind had channeled down the canyon, smashing all before it.

The fire was built of dry wood, the aspens' leaves would dissipate the smoke, and the outcropping of rock would shield their fire from observation. It was a good position, but there were many such. All a man needed to do was keep his eyes open and know what he was looking for.

All through the west country he knew of such places, most of which he had never used, but all were filed away in his memory for such a time as they might be needed.

Con Vallian had learned long since there was little that was original in this. Almost any camp you chose had been chosen before, many times, and nearly always one found the remains of old fires, arrowheads, spear-points or even the crudest of stone axes.

Con Vallian used his Bowie to gather boughs for a bed for McKaskel. When he had it made he spread his own bed on it. "You ain't going to be much use for a few days, Mac," he commented, so you better rest up. I'll he'p your folks make out until you're up and around."

"I can't thank you enough, Vallian. This is mighty fine of you."

"Neighbors, sort of. Out here we set store by neighbors. Count them a blessing."

"But you are not our neighbor," Tom said. "Not really."

"Depends. All depends. Out here most anybody in a hundred miles is a neighbor. Folks are more scattered out. On the other hand, I don't know as anybody ever set limits on the word. My ma used to say anybody who was in need was a neighbor."

As he talked, Con worked, cutting boughs for more beds, bringing in fuel for the night's fire, pausing only occasionally to listen.

He liked the smell of the smoke, like the effect the sunset had on the leaves. He listened, and heard the rustle of the water in the creek nearby, heard a faint stirring in the leaves as a squirrel hunted for food. He stood up, and taking his rifle said, "I'll be back. There's grub in my saddlebags, but go easy. No tellin' when we'll get more."

Con Vallian disappeared into the trees, parallel to the way they had come.

"His father must have been a well-educated man," Susanna commented, when he had gone.

Susanna knelt beside the fire, stirring a little broth made from jerky. Their only utensil was Con's cup.

A cool wind fluttered the leaves, and moaned softly in the pines. Tom came in with an armful of wood for the fire. "It's getting dark out there," he said. "Pa? Will bears come up to a fire?"

"I don't think so, son. Most animals are afraid of fire, and afraid of the man-smell."

Susanna glanced at him. "Did you hear something, Tom?"

The boy shrugged. "You always hear things in the woods. There's always some kind of a sound out there. Mr. Vallian says you have to listen for the usual sounds until your ears only pick out the unusual. I am not very good at that yet."

The flames fluttered. Susanna glanced over at her husband. He was quiet now, his eyes closed, but still awake. He must be in pain, but he showed none of it. Suddenly she was very proud of him. But she was frightened, too. There was no telling when Vallian would ride off again, and they were alone in the woods, and Duncan was hurt. It would be days . . . perhaps several weeks . . . before he could ride again, or even walk.

"Tom? Keep Pa's rifle close by. I have the shotgun."

"I wonder if they took our powder and lead? We'll need it, Ma. I didn't figure on being out more than an hour or two."

"Have you got much?"

"Not more than eight or ten charges for the rifle, and I don't think Pa has more loads than he's carrying in the pistol."

Con Vallian moved along the edge of the woods, testing each step as he put the foot down for fear of a fallen branch. He favored moccasins for woods work, and usually carried some, but his last had worn out and he'd not gotten a squaw to make a new pair for him. Those Injuns yonder on the plains. They would have done it. They were good folks . . . unless you met them on a war party.

When he was well away from even the smallest sounds of the camp he paused and began to sift the night-movements with his ears. A branch rubbing against another, leaves rustling, something, a bird or squirrel or rabbit, maybe, rustling a nest into the leaves. He listened and decided all was well here, but then he moved on, walking on cat feet.

The stars were out but clouds were scattered. There was a high wind tonight. He was up wind of their camp, testing for smoke. There was none.

That did not mean there was no cause to worry. The Shabbitt outfit might be very close and lying quiet. He looked back toward the camp, but could see nothing. The place was hidden, and approaching it would be difficult because of the enormous number of fallen trees from the blow-down. New trees had grown up, some of them towering up to forty to fifty feet, but the old trunks lay in a maze. Even by daylight a horseman could not penetrate that barrier, nor could a man on foot move with any speed.

Gloomily, he stared down the long meadow, gray in the starlight. Something moved down there.

A vague movement . . . bear, maybe.

He stood still, waiting. Duncan McKaskel ought to go back to that cabin. That was a right nice place . . . water close by, and meadows for cattle. There were beaver in those ponds and where there was beaver there were fish, and all manner of wild life. Elk favored aspens, and there were aspens aplenty around that cabin.

No more movement down there . . . the wind was from him toward the lower end of the meadow and if it was a bear or elk they had his scent by now.

Why was he here, anyway? What did he want with those eastern folks? They were no kin. He hadn't never seen them until he drank their coffee that morning . . . it was good coffee, all right.

He looked away from the end of the meadow, letting the corner of his eyes hold sight of it.

The corners of the eyes were sometimes better for locating movement.

Yes . . . there was something down there. Maybe fifty yards off . . . no, it would be further. His ears caught no sound but whatever was down there was coming closer.

His clothing was neutral in color, his body would fade into the trees behind him, so he waited. His fingers went to the Bowie. It was a good weapon at night, and a shot might bring that whole outfit down on him. Anyway, it might be an animal . . . only he no longer believed that.

He waited, unmoving yet prepared. Whoever approached was coming along as silently as he himself had moved. Was it the Huron? Con crouched low, trying to hear any slightest movement in the grass, remembering his father's stories of the Iroquois, deadly enemy of the Huron Indians, and how they had decimated the Iroquois in the battles that followed the arrival of the French.

Con Vallian listened straining all his attention to hear. He had met the Huron only once, and had nearly lost his life. But this time—

There was a whisper of feet in the grass, a sudden rush from the night, starlight on a blade.

He threw himself to one side and felt the cold steel of the blade as it grazed him. His rifle in his left hand, he hit low and hard and up with the blade. It struck, something ripped and then he was hit hard on the shoulder. He rolled back, throwing up his feet to catch the Huron as he dove at him. His feet churned, smashing hard into his attacker's face, and then he was up, swinging his rifle with both hands.

It hit nothing but empty air. He dropped, groping for his fallen knife, and then he moved swiftly, silently off to his left, holding the rifle before him like a sword to guard off a sudden attack. Again the rush of feet. He dropped to his knees and the Huron spilled over him. He thrust hard with his knife again and again . . . nothing.

Dammit, where *was* the man? Even as the thought flickered in his consciousness, a shadow loomed before him, striking his rifle aside, lunging at him again.

Vallian struck the side of the attacker's head with his fist. He felt the Huron stagger under the blow. He struck again, but the Indian was gone. Crouching, gasping for breath, Vallian waited, every sense alert, for the next attack.

He waited, then slowly straightened up.

All was still. Overhead were the stars in a vast and empty sky. The wind stirred the grass and the aspen leaves whispered mysterious sounds. Slowly his breathing slowed. The Huron—and it had surely been he—was gone.

Dropping to one knee he felt for his rifle and found it, then got up slowly.

"Damn!" he whispered softly. "Dammit to Hell!"

For the first time in his life he wanted to kill a man, and for the first time in a long while, he knew he was afraid.

Chapter XV

When Con Vallian moved off into the night, Susanna listened to the faint sounds that lasted only as long as there was a shadow of him, and then they stilled. He was gone.

Duncan had finished his broth, and fallen asleep. Once, when he started to move, he moaned softly, and she felt fear go through her like a chill.

What if he had been injured internally? He had taken a bad fall, and would be relatively helpless for a time. What if she should be left alone here, with Tom?

It was a frightening thought. She was independent of mind but Duncan had always been there, as her father before him. Without him, in this wilderness, what could she do?

Her independence, she suddenly realized, had not in fact been independence at all, for she had depended on the law, on society, on all those things that gave her freedom and entitled her to respect. And out here there was none of that. Out here she was alone.

The firelight moved weird witch-shadows against the darkness, and a soft wind came through the leaves, fluttering the fire. Duncan muttered in his sleep, and she glanced to where Tom lay. He was also asleep, curled against the faint chill.

Susanna added sticks to the fire, then looked again to the shotgun. There were two shells in the barrels and she had two more in her pockets. It was little enough.

They had left everything back at the cabin. What if it was destroyed? Duncan had only a little money.

She looked into the fire, loving the warmth and the hot coals that now lay in its bed. Fortunately there was no end of fuel.

Something stirred in the forest and she felt the skin prickle along the back of her neck. She glanced toward the shotgun. It was over there, out of reach . . . how could she be such a fool? Con Vallian never moved without his rifle. It was almost an extension of himself, and now she knew why.

She straightened up from the fire, adding a few sticks, as she did so, then she drew her shoulders together as if experiencing a chill. She went to the blankets as if to pick up her coat. Instead she took up the shotgun and turned.

A man was standing at the edge of the firelight. It was the dark man in the buckskin jacket, the one who had been with the flat-nosed man at the cabin.

"How do you do?" she said quietly. "Is there something I can do for you?"

His eyes went from her to the man. "He is not well?"

"Yes, he has been hurt. A lion jumped on his horse. He was thrown."

"That was very clever . . . with the shotgun."

"I am learning."

He laughed, suddenly, pleasantly. "Yes . . . yes, I think you are."

"Who is he? That other man?"

"A friend. He has been very helpful."

The Huron came a step further. *"Who* is he? I must know."

There was a deep cut on the Huron's cheekbone, and his buckskin jacket had been slashed.

"Are you hurt? Your face seems to be cut."

"It is nothing. Tell me who he is."

"His name is Con Vallian."

"Ahh!" The sound was a sudden, sharp exhalation, startling in its intensity. "You tell him this for me, that next time I shall kill him."

"Why? Why should you kill him? Or anybody? Isn't that rather savage?"

He turned his attention to her. "I am a savage. I am the Huron."

"I do not think you are a savage. When you came to the cabin it was you who spoke for me. That man . . . the other man. If you had not spoken there might have been trouble."

"Red Hyle would have killed him. He has spoken for you."

"He has? You may tell Mr. Hyle that I am married, happily married."

The Huron looked at her thoughtfully. "Hyle would kill him. He would kill your husband. Then he would take you."

"And you would let him?"

"Why not? What are you to me?"

"I am a woman. You are a gentleman."

For the first time there was a shadow of a smile on his face. "You are clever, to put that burden upon me, but ask anyone and they will tell you the Huron is a savage. Ask your friend."

"Mr. Vallian?" She indicated his face. "Did he do that?"

"It was our second meeting. I thought I had killed him the first time. I look forward to the third."

"He is a good man, Huron."

"I think so. But I will kill him. Nobody escapes the Huron twice."

Suddenly, he was gone.

She stood staring, then turned swiftly. Con Vallian was walking into camp. He paused, looking beyond her. "I thought I heard someone talking."

"It was the Huron."

"*Here?*" Vallian stared at her. "You were talking with him?"

"He speaks very well . . . excellent English. I thought there was a shadow of French, but I cannot be sure."

"Well, I'll be damned."

"You had better eat, Mr. Vallian."

He glanced at McKaskel. "How is he?"

"In some pain, I think, but he is sleeping. I fed him some broth."

So the Huron had been here and knew their location. Would he bring the others? It was likely, but then one never could outguess the Huron.

"What are you thinking of?"

"That Injun . . . next time we meet one of us will get killed. He moves like a ghost. Makes a man right uneasy, with him around. The first time he almost killed me."

He ate the food she gave him, yet there was a restlessness about him, an unease. Twice the Huron had come upon him unheard, something he believed no man could do. He got up suddenly. "We're going back."

"Back?"

"To your cabin. You had decided to stay there, and it is a good place. They may come back looking for you, and they may not, but there is a time to stop running, and the time is now, the place is there."

With help they got McKaskel into the saddle. Con Vallian led the way, not along the dim trail by which they had come, but up through the aspens, on a winding route among the trees. Suddenly they emerged on the slope of the mountain. Below them, bathed in moonlight now, lay a wide flat, a high, grassy plateau.

They crossed it at a gallop, then entered the trees

once more, weaving among them through the filtered moonlight. The rain had softened the leaves under foot and their horses made little sound. When they came at last to the cabins it was upstream, from below. They were under the cottonwoods.

Near the house they saw their wagon, and Con stopped them. "I'll go up there," he said.

There was no way to approach the house under cover, so he walked his horse across the meadow to the cabin, watching the house and prepared for anything. Nothing happened.

The door swung on hinges, and nothing seemed disturbed. "Better get some sleep."

"We left the other mules in a corral." Tom pointed. "It's back there."

"You get some sleep. I'll have a look at them."

Susanna turned at the door. "You will stay? You will be here in the morning?"

"I'll stay."

He walked away, pausing only when he was in the blackness under the trees. He turned to glance around. It was a good place they had chosen.

He found the corral and it was what he had supposed. The original owner of the cabin had simply pulled dead-falls into place among the close-growing aspens to form a crude fence. Probably the little he had done had been done from horseback, simply swinging logs into a better position. Yet it permitted a nice bit of grass and grazing for the mules.

He had no idea how the showdown would come. Now that they knew he was here it might be approached more carefully, for they would know about Con Vallian.

But seven of them? Duncan McKaskel would be a help, and so would the others, but they'd be better off holed up in the cabin. For himself, he preferred to be outside. He had always believed in a war of movement, and was not given to occupying static positions.

Standing in the shadows near the cabin, he studied the layout. The approach from the creek could be covered by fire from the house, and so could the trail down from the bench. Except for the windows, nobody was going to get a bullet into that house . . . well, the door was a risk, but a lesser one.

The dangerous area was near the bench where land broke off sharply and dropped away to the area of the beaver-dams. A rifleman, or several of them, could get close to the house from there and there would be no way to smoke them out.

Con Vallian looked from the bank across the beaver ponds and the naked tree trunks lying on the green and marshy ground. Beyond were the still pools where the beaver had gathered water.

It was a good place the McKaskels had chosen, rich with the quiet of trees and still water. Over there, just down the way a bit was the river, running pleasantly over the stones.

Once a man had been here, perhaps with a family. He had seen and loved this place and had built this cabin, and then somehow he had gone away. Had he tired of it? Had he fallen and died? Been killed by Indians or renegades? Did he lie buried in some mine tunnel only he himself knew? Or had he simply gone off to Cherry Creek, which people were beginning to call Denver, and never come back?

Susanna came out from the house. "Are you listening? Should I be quiet?"

He shrugged. "I was thinking that this is the best life, always the best. I was thinking that cities are no place for men."

"You may be right, Mr. Vallian, but cities have much to offer. They have better educational advantages, and culture."

"Maybe. I wouldn't be knowin' about such things."

"Do you think they'll come tonight?"

"Doubt it. But I'll never try to outguess that Huron. He's a canny one, and the next time they come, ma'am, it'll be root hog or die, no two ways about it."

Vallian pushed his hat back. "You're fresh out of the eastern lands, so get it straight in your minds. When they come back they'll be killin'. No matter if they say, 'you do this an' you'll get off scot-free', or 'do that an' we'll not harm your boy,' Ma'am, don't you believe them.

"When a man starts out to do violence there's only one way. You got to defend yourselves.

"Now these men. Purdy's a bad one, but he might give you a break. His brother Ike wouldn't even give Purdy a break, and neither would Red Hyle. Doc Shabbitt is mean, dirty, and a coward, but he'll kill you just as quick, an' the others gather someplace between."

"I . . . I wanted a home out here, Mr. Vallian. I did not think I'd have to fight for it."

"No, ma'am, but you have to fight for most of the things worth havin' . . . or somebody does."

Chapter XVI

For a time Con Vallian walked about, gathering sticks, hauling dead-falls closer to the house, building up a pile of wood for the fire. He had always enjoyed working with his hands. Moreover, he thought better while working.

There were seven tough men in Shabbitt's lot, as opposed to McKaskel and himself. Susanna and Tom would fire some, would load for them, and could be helpful, yet he had to find some way of shortening the odds.

He was not a man who wanted to kill, yet the men he had to face had no such compunctions. He doubted whether any of them actually liked to kill, unless it was Ike Mantle but the others did it just the same.

Aside from Hyle or Purdy Mantle, Con doubted whether any of them would stand up to a man in a fair fight. The trouble was, they could choose their time and their direction.

Con Vallian did not like the idea of fighting from a

position, such as the cabin. He preferred to be outside, under the trees.

He paused, straightening up and leaning on the thick
branch he held in his hand. Slowly he surveyed the
area.

They might be already out there, watching. But suppose they were not? Suppose instead of waiting inside
the cabin for an attack, they waited outside?

The attackers could come across the stream, down
from the bench, or they could come downstream. The
only other route was across the beaver ponds. Possible, but difficult owing to the great number of fallen
trees and the marshy ground.

If they came downstream they must hold fairly close
to the banks where there were dim trails or at least
openings among the trees and brush.

Con walked to the woodpile and threw the branch
on it, then walked upstream about thirty yards and
stopped.

If this was their route they would be confined in a
space some forty or fifty yards across. Elsewhere they'd
be in the river-bottom where the sound of horses' hoofs
on stones would give too much advance warning of
their coming.

On his right, before one reached the bank, there
was thick brush. Some trees, their roots still clinging
to the bank above, leaned far out, shading the brush.
Before the thick stand of brush were several rotting
trees, fallen long years ago, their broken stumps all
that remained.

He walked up to the brush. Peering through the
slender trunks of the trees, he could see a small open
space where some animal had bedded down. The brush
along the bank above was impenetrable for anything
larger than a bobcat.

The brush where the trees leaned over was actually
a thick stand of aspens, few of them more than three
inches in diameter, none exceeding five inches. As with
all such stands, a number of trees had already died
and fallen, their slender trunks criss-crossing among

the waist-high brush that skirted the aspens and grew among the outer fringe of trees.

Con walked back to the house. "Put a little jerky together, some coffee and such-like. We're going to camp out tonight."

"Camp out?"

"Leave the fire burning and a couple of good logs that will last the night. Eat up now, and let's move out. Bring your guns and all the ammunition."

"Now, see here!" McKaskel objected. "I'm in no shape—"

"I'll help you. We're going to sleep yonder tonight."

A half hour later, a tarpaulin rigged to keep out the rain, they were bedded down in the aspen. From inside there was more room than it appeared, for the back had a considerable overhang.

From their hiding place they had an excellent view of the cabin and all the area around it.

"Good!" McKaskel said. "Excellent!"

"This here's for you. They'll try slippin' in close, so you've got to be quiet. When you see one of them . . . shoot."

"Without warning?"

"Why not? They'd do it to you, and this here isn't any war for prisoners. You're thinkin' about stayin' alive, ma'am, and what if you got the drop on one of them and told him to put his hands up and he did? What would you do with him? There's no law to turn him over to, no jail to hold him."

"Where will you be?"

Con Vallian hitched his gun-belt. "I'm goin' huntin', ma'am. I figure to whittle 'em down a mite."

"Be careful."

He moved off quickly into the aspens. He would be careful, all right. With that Huron around he'd have to be.

Con Vallian had no idea of taking prisoners himself, but if he could put one or more of them out of action, it would shorten the odds.

When he was well away he glanced back. Certainly,

no better place could have been chosen, for it was the least likely spot. It seemed to offer nothing, to be merely a narrow wall of brush at the foot of the bank that marked the river-bottom.

He moved quickly to the denser woods. This was no time for a horse. He wished again for moccasins, but had none, and moved almost as quietly in boots, putting each foot down carefully, avoiding broken branches and stiff brush that could scratch against clothes.

He squatted near some rocks in view of the cabin. It was dusk and the stark outlines of things were beginning to blend into one common darkness. He could see the grassy bottom where the old corral stood, but nothing moved. Once something brushed leaves near him and a deer passed within a few yards, unaware of his presence.

Red Hyle held a cup in his hands and sipped coffee. His powerful legs were spread wide, his boots planted solidly. He looked massive, immovable. "Vallian, is it? I've heard of him."

"So have we all," Purdy commented dryly. "He's good. Damned good."

"Maybe she lied," Johnny Dobbs suggested. "Maybe she was tryin' to scare us off."

"Who's scared?" Ike scoffed. "Vallian's only one man."

"He's a good one," Purdy said. "Maybe he's the best."

Red Hyle looked up sharply, staring at Purdy, and Purdy grinned at him. "Exceptin' Hyle, here. Red could take him."

Red stared at him. "Or maybe you could?" he sneered.

Purdy shrugged. "I'm not looking to . . . unless he crosses me. I think we'd better set back an' take a long look at this here situation. What we got to decide is, is it worth it?"

"We could ride on to Cherry Creek. Miners come

down from the diggin's, loaded for bear. It should be easy, real easy."

"I owe that woman," Booster objected. "It was her hit me. I'd bet on it."

Doc Shabbitt was silent. One way to remain a leader was to let the wind blow, then get ahead of it. Johnny was ready to pull out, and Purdy would vote that way, he was sure. Doc wanted Vallian dead for killing Lenny, but that could wait, and if he waited maybe Red would do it.

"Look at it," Purdy said quietly. "We've lost two men. Lenny dead, and Pangman surely is, even if we never seen his body. Two dead and nothing to show, an' now we know Vallian is in it. I say we study this matter."

Hyle turned his head. "Where'd you see them, Huron?"

"There . . . ," the Huron gestured vaguely. "I do not think they will be there now."

"Gone to Cherry Creek, maybe?" Booster suggested.

"An' leave their wagon?" Ike asked. "They'll come back. Anyway, I figure they want to settle down, claim that land."

Hyle got up. "We'll ride down to the cabin." He glanced around, his eyes cold. "We'll all go."

"Of course," Doc agreed easily, "wasn't that what we planned?"

One by one they went to their horses. Ike quickly, Purdy, smiling. Booster lagged a little, but tightened his cinch. "How far is it?" he asked.

"Three, four miles. Take us an hour, I figure, in the dark and all."

"You figure to tackle Vallian in the dark?" Booster asked.

Purdy shrugged. "I wouldn't take him away from Red," he said, "Red Hyle can take him, and I know he wants him."

Red Hyle said nothing. Purdy smiled to himself. *He'll turn his back on me, but he never would on Ike . . . not if they'd had words.*

"We'll wait until daybreak," Shabbitt said. "We'll move just before it gets light."

Nobody argued the point. They swung to the saddle and walked their horses south to be within easy striking range of the cabin.

"Noticed a place," Shabbitt said, "about a mile this side."

They rode without talking, a surly silence of men without allegiance or loyalty, no one sure of he who rode beside him.

The place Doc led them to was just a hollow in the trees near the creek. It was shaped well for concealment and nobody would be apt to come up on them unexpectedly, even if anyone had been traveling this way, and no one was.

They tied their horses close and built a small fire. Red Hyle dealt a game of solitaire and Purdy napped against a tree. Doc Shabbitt stared into the flames, chewing on the stub of a cigar, while Ike Mantle slept and Booster stirred the fire, smoked innumerable cigarettes. The Huron sat cross-legged at one side, staring into the fire.

Johnny Dobbs stretched and yawned. Why did he ever get hooked up with this Shabbitt outfit? Damn it! What he really wanted to do was sleep. He'd like to go back to the fire and stretch out for a good night's sleep.

The voice behind him was low, confidential. "Don't turn around, my friend, because if you do I'll have to kill you."

"I ain't movin'."

"I'm Con Vallian, Dobbs. I knew you from away back. I am givin' you a chance to show some judgment. I'm givin' you a chance to fade out."

"And if I don't?"

"You'll be the first man I'll kill. I think you know me, Dobbs, and even if you get away I'll follow you down and shoot you on sight."

"I ain't scared. I ain't a bit scared . . . same time,

I'd as soon get shut of this deal. It ain't my kind of a show."

"My feeling exactly, Dobbs. Well, you ridin'?"

Dobbs' mind scurried like a cornered rat, hunting any way out. "Look, I can't get my horse. They'd kill me. Give me a break an' I'll fall back and light out like a scared rabbit."

"All right, Dobbs. Either way you choose, this here is good-bye."

Dobbs hesitated. "Good-bye," he said quickly, and he meant it.

Chapter XVII

Con Vallian was laboring under no delusions. Dobbs might and might not do as he had said, but knowing the man Con believed he would if he could. Dobbs would rustle a few head here and there but Con had heard nothing about Dobbs that indicated he was vicious or brutal.

Con returned to his horse and waited there, thinking out the situation. If the Shabbitt outfit rode right in as expected, and if Duncan McKaskel would shoot from ambush there was every chance the odds might be cut drastically. Of the two Susanna was more apt to shoot than Duncan.

Nobody needed to draw any pictures for Susanna. She had seen those men when she came through town, they had tried then to kill her husband, and attack their camp. Susanna had discarded lady-like restraint when she bashed Booster McCutcheon across the nose with a club.

Con chuckled. Well, one thing about her. When she decided to swing she really laid it in there with both hands.

What now?

They had moved up to be within striking distance, and this time they would be coming for blood. They had had a long trek across country, had run into trouble, had their numbers trimmed down somewhat, and were in no mood for trifling.

Then there was the Huron.

Con debated approaching their camp, but the Huron had ears like a cat, and a sixth sense that might warn him of any movement he did not otherwise detect. It was foolish to ask for trouble.

He mounted, then walked his horse away along the stream, making almost no sound on the soft earth. From time to time he paused to listen. Finally, he rode to the hidden corral among the aspen where McKaskel kept his mules.

All was still. He left his horse in the deepest shadow, and taking his rifle moved out to a point on the bank where he could cover the open ground near the cabin, and then he waited.

The night was still. He could hear the rustling of the water from the creek, a faint stirring among the leaves, and once he glimpsed a night-hawk diving and swirling in the air above him. He wiped his palms on his shirt front and took up his rifle again.

Something moved! The faintest shadow of movement, near the cabin! He eased his position a little, lying stretched out on the ground, and slowly put the rifle on target, digging his left elbow into the soft loam. He was glad he had a cartridge in the chamber for the sound of loading would be sharp and clear on such a night, in such a place.

There was a faint light from the cabin, a flickering of fire from the hearth. Somebody or something was checking the cabin.

He shifted his gaze, letting his eyes roam over the open ground before the cabin, down to the trees along the stream, and then he saw them.

They were not coming as he had expected, riding in a tight group down the trail, but were coming from the trees in a skirmish line, and they were walking their horses. Only a faint stirring in the dark warned him, only a suggestion of movement.

He shot a quick glance toward the cabin. The Huron? Perhaps . . . but gone now.

He looked back, praying that McKaskel was alert, for the renegades were scattered and moving with almost no sound. Nor were they clearly visible.

Turning slightly he brought his rifle to bear, tried to estimate the height and distance, then aimed where he believed a rider's body would be. He let his finger tighten slowly on the trigger, and then the rifle leaped and the sharp report split the night. From below there was a sudden wild yell, and the horsemen charged.

On the instant another rifle bellowed from the McKaskel position, and a man cried out, then swore. Another shot . . . Con had rolled over three times, now he held his fire, waiting for a shot from the attackers.

They had vanished.

A sudden rush on discovery, a scattering, and a few return shots, fired at random. One bullet had struck the earth near him, another ricocheted off a branch above his head.

He pulled back quickly, moved down slope on the steep bank, and crouched among the young trees, waiting. A man lay sprawled on the grass down there. His riderless horse had run off across the stream.

They had charged the house, circled swiftly as they realized their mistake, and were now scattered, undoubtedly stalking him and McKaskel as well.

How many were out of it? Only the one? And was he done for, or merely lying quiet until he could make a dash for shelter?

Con eased back a little under the trees. They had offered no shelter and only a slight concealment, but the field of fire had been excellent.

Who was down? So much could depend on that. If it was Red Hyle . . . or Purdy. Small chance!

He worked his way down the steep slope among the trees until he reached the level of the cabin. At least two of the attackers had gone over the edge into the area around the beaver ponds. There was soft ground there, with scattered logs, as well as much standing timber, gray and ghost-like in the pale light of the moon.

Suddenly, McKaskel or someone from the ambush, fired.

Instantly four or five rifles replied, riddling the trees and brush with lead. Con swore at the action, but took the opportunity. He fired quickly at the nearest flash. Shifting his rifle, he shot again at a point where another shot had come from.

A bullet clipped leaves above his head. He fired again, at the flash, then slid swiftly through the brush, working his way to the edge of the beaver ponds.

There, except for the standing trees which were scattered, there was little cover. The fallen trees were old and bare. He hesitated, then moved out among them, working his way toward the other side. Twice he had to crouch behind an old dead stump when he heard movement. He also heard someone swear, and the muttering of a man in pain.

He could distinguish nothing, nor could he hear a voice clearly enough to place it.

His foot slipped as he crossed a narrow stretch of sand and his boot came down on stone. He slipped, and the boot went into the water.

A bullet clipped a chip from a log almost at his feet, and he took a long step, merging with a narrow-leafed cottonwood on the bank. He had crossed the ponds, and now—

Nothing happened.

Near the bases of the trees there were long dark piles of dead branches, logs, slabs of bark—refuse left by the last high water or, perhaps by the floods over the years. He crouched near them, watching for some movement.

Suddenly, off to his left he heard the pounding of

hoofs. Men had ridden away. At least two, probably more.

A trick? A device to get him to stand up and move so he could be killed? Or had they abandoned the fight?

He waited while the minutes went slowly by. There was no other sound, not so much as a whisper of movement. An owl swung low over the beaver ponds and winged by, unalarmed. Still, he remained where he was.

After a while he moved stealthily forward, waited, then moved again. There was nothing, no sound, no movement.

Suddenly, from further off, he heard another horse, a lone rider this time, start off. Hoofbeats dwindled and the sound faded out.

From where he now stood he could see a horse standing with an empty saddle. He could see the reflected light from the polished leather. Out on the grass some thirty yards from the cabin he could see the dark shape of what appeared to be a body.

Warily he moved around through the trees, doubly careful, for he was now in enemy country and did not wish to be shot by McKaskel.

By the time another half hour had gone by he had worked his way around the ambush position, and then slipped through the slender white aspens to the place of ambush.

It was empty. They were gone.

In the darkness he could see nothing. Squatting, he ran his fingers swiftly over the leaves that had been the wild animal bed. Nothing . . . no blood, no weapons, no bodies.

Why had they pulled out? Or had they been taken by force?

To move around searching would be to wipe out what sign they might have left, so he pulled back and strode across the moonlit grass toward the fallen man.

With a boot toe, he rolled him over. The man's hat fell off, and his face turned up to the sky.

Booster McCutcheon, with a bullet hole through his skull and his body caked with blood from other wounds.

He stopped at McCutcheon's horse. Then mounting he rode back around the cabin to the hidden mule corral. The mules were still there, and the sorrel horses as well as his own. He stripped the gear from Booster's horse and turned it in with the others, then led out his own horse and stepped into the saddle.

At this moment there was little he could do, except to avoid smearing what tracks they might have left. Two possibilities remained. Either Red Hyle and Doc Shabbitt had captured the McKaskels, or being doubtful of their position, the McKaskels had themselves pulled out.

If the first were true Red would not bother with Mc-Kaskel. He would kill him and leave him where he fell.

Unless the others still believed in the gold, and hoped to torture the hiding place from him. And they would not believe him when he denied there was any gold.

The Mantles were still around, no doubt, and the Huron. He walked his horse into the edge of the aspens and tying the horse, he stretched out on the ground and slept. He was dead tired, and he slept soundly, watched over by the mustang.

Nearby the stream rustled, above him the aspens whispered mysteriously of the night and an owl spoke inquiringly at the moon.

Duncan McKaskel had decided quickly, after the first burst of firing.

By then, he decided, the attackers would know their position, and would move in swiftly. Hence the logical move was to get out.

He whispered his decision to Susanna and Tom.

"Pa!" Tom said excitedly, "There's a path up the

bank right here! I found it! You can go right up through the trees!"

"Let's have a look."

At some time in the past deer had evidently come down the bank under cover of the trees. Possibly it had been those very deer who had slept here, but regardless of that, it offered a covered escape route by which they could leave the ambush position without being seen.

"All right, Tom. You take your mother up that trail. Follow right along where the deer went and cross the open place up there to the trees across the way. You wait there for me."

"Duncan? What about you?" Susanna asked.

"Don't worry. I'll wait, fire a few more shots, then get out. That will make them think we're still here."

"And if we miss each other? What then?"

"Go to the hidden corral, where we left the mules."

Tom tugged at his mother's arm. "Ma! Come on!"

Reluctantly, with a quick glance over her shoulder, she followed.

Bright as the moonlight was out in the open, it was dark and still back under the close-growing aspens. The path was steep and even darker. Holding her skirts away from the brush, Susanna followed Tom. It was only a dozen yards or so to the top of the bank.

Tom looked quickly around, found the way the deer had gone. Tom grabbed his mother's arm. Swiftly, they moved along the trail.

Duncan McKaskel looked out into the moonlit clearing. A tall man in a slope-brimmed slouch hat was standing there with a gun in his hand. The man's face was invisible, but there was no doubt that he was one of the renegades.

"Howdy, Mac. Was you goin' to go some wheres?"

Duncan McKaskel had expected to be frightened, and he supposed he was. These men were not the sort to hesitate over a killing. He knew that. "Not really," he spoke quietly, stalling for time, for any kind of a break. "I was looking forward to a talk with you."

"With me?" The man was obviously startled.

"Why, of course. I am a curious man, Mr. . . . ah?"

"Mantle. Ike Mantle."

"I am a curious man, Mr. Mantle, and ever since this all began I have been curious. I have been wondering why you were following me. If you don't mind, it did seem rather pointless."

Ike Mantle was puzzled, and he was curious, also. This man was different, somehow. He was a tenderfoot—everybody knew that—but he was different.

"Ain't so hard to figger," he said conversationally, "we wanted your gold."

"Gold?" Duncan McKaskel was startled. "But I have no gold. Lord, man, if I had gold do you suppose I'd ever leave all that back east and come out here? I don't know if you've been east—"

"I ain't."

"What I mean is there's a dozen ways to enjoy money back there for every one out here. If I had any gold I'd of stayed there until I spent it." He paused. "In fact, that's just what I did, I am afraid. I never had much but what I had just seemed to dribble away."

Ike understood. "I reckon it'll do that wherever you are." Then the fact touched him and stirred him to irritation. "You mean you got nothing in that wagon?"

"We did have some of Susanna . . . that's Mrs. McKaskel . . . we did have some of her furniture, but the load was too heavy. About all that's left now are a few tools, our bedding, and what we need to live. You know, a small sheet-iron stove, Dutch oven, and such things."

"Well," Ike said resignedly, "you got mules, horses, and your woman. We'll have to settle for that."

Ike was rather amazed with himself. Here he was talking things over with a man he fully intended to kill, but it was McKaskel's approach that threw him,

the easy, conversational way that invited the same
sort of reaction.

"Why don't you just ride off, Mr. Mantle? Look,
those horses and mules will do you nothing but harm.
They are known, Mr. Mantle."

"Don't matter. Ain't no law out here that doesn't
come from the barrel of a six-gun, and mine's as
good as any other."

"There's a rope, Mr. Mantle. I have heard it said
that quite a lot of law is enforced with a rope. Par-
ticularly where a woman is involved . . . or the steal-
ing of horses."

"Who'll know?" Ike said. "Horses are horses an'
mules are mules, and you folks . . . you won't be
givin' evidence agin us."

"Mr. Mantle? Why don't you fellows just ride out
of here and forget all this? You thought we had
gold. We have none. Our wagon has nothing that would
be of value to riding men, and I must warn you. Our
mules and the sorrels would be a death-trap for you."

"A death-trap? What's that mean?"

Duncan McKaskel lied quietly, coolly. "Mr. Mantle, my brother is in Cherry Creek. He is an officer
in the cavalry there. There are, I believe, three troops
of cavalry stationed near there at this moment because
of expected Indian trouble. My brother is expecting
us. When we do not arrive on time, and we are already several days late, he will be curious.

"My brother is a very hard, persistent man. He
will begin to look around. Those mules and the sorrels
were purchased from my brother, who raised them
himself. As you have noticed, these are no ordinary
sort of mules, and the sorrels are well bred. He will
start looking for those horses, and he will find you and
your friends.

"I might add, sir, that my brother is a very pre-
cipitate sort of a man. I mean, when angered he acts
quickly, and he will have several hundred soldiers to
help him."

It was a good story, and McKaskel wished it were true.

"You!" Ike Mantle gestured with his gun. "Walk out there in the open." McKaskel walked. "Now right . . . into the trees."

They were waiting for him.

"Where's the woman?" Hyle demanded. "Where is she?"

"Gone. They done pulled out. I caught this one as he figured to go after 'em."

"I'll kill the—!"

"Hold up there!" Ike threw up a hand. "You pull in your neck, Red. This here's my prisoner. Anyway, you better hear what he told me."

Ike repeated the story, with some trimmings, and Doc Shabbitt swore. "Hell, Ike! He's lyin'! Can't you see that?"

"Mebbe. But you want to ride into Cherry Crick with them mules and find out you're wrong? They hung a man over there a few weeks ago. They'll do it. That there's a rough bunch."

"Where's your woman?" Red thrust himself at McKaskel. "Where'd she go, damn it!"

"I haven't the slightest idea, and if I knew, I would not tell you."

Red swung a wicked backhand blow that knocked him sprawling. McKaskel hit the ground with a jolt, his head spinning, the taste of blood in his mouth. He had been hit before. He had been a boxer and it was his instinct to get up. He started up and looked at three guns.

Slowly, he got to his feet.

"She's with Vallian," he said, and spat blood. "She left me."

Chapter XVIII

Even as he lied he hoped she was with Vallian, for with him she would be safe . . . safer, anyway. He put the back of his hand against his smashed lip and stared at the blood. He could feel something happening within him.

He had been a peace-loving man. He believed in peace, had argued for it, written about it. There was no difficulty he had said, that could not be solved without violence by reasonable human beings. That was what he had said, and what he now believed. Or had believed until now.

"We have no reason for trouble," he said quietly. "As I was explaining to Mr. Mantle, I have nothing of value. That was the reason I came west, to start over again."

"Was that true? What you said about your brother and troops in Cherry Creek?" Shabbitt demanded.

"Why else would I have said it?" he replied. "But even if it were not true you know what the attitude would be toward such an attack as this."

"Kill him," Ike Mantle said, after a moment. "Kill him and let's get out of here."

"Why bother?" Purdy wanted to know. "Just turn him loose. He's got no horse, an' he's a tenderfoot. There's Utes all over this country who'd take his hair."

"Build a fire," Shabbitt said suddenly. "I want some coffee. No use tryin' to trace 'em down until daylight, anyway."

Purdy looked at McKaskel. "You say Vallian's got your woman?"

"She's gone, isn't she? And so's he. They even took my boy."

"I wondered why he was hangin' around," Shabbitt said. "Begins to make sense." Doc glanced around at Red Hyle. "He beat you to it, Red."

Hyle shrugged.

Purdy began to gather sticks and put a fire together. He broke some bark from a dead stump and shredded it between his palms to use for tinder. It caught quickly when he held a match to it, and flared up. He added some thin tissues of bark, then twigs.

Ike walked to his horse and got a coffee-pot and came back. "He ain't worth nothin'. We can kill him or leave him."

"Somethin' funny here," Shabbitt said. "If'n Con Vallian stole his woman, why ain't he sore? Why ain't he after him?"

"Turn me loose," McKaskel said. "Give me a chance."

"You want to go after him?" Purdy asked.

"Well, I would have to consider it. Con Vallian is a dead shot. I'd have to make up my mind whether I'd trade my life for a woman. There's other women, but I've only one life."

"It makes sense," Purdy agreed.

Nobody else spoke. The night air was cold and they moved closer to the fire. Duncan McKaskel decided to hold his peace. For the time they seemed to have forgotten him, and to have forgotten their intention to kill him. Yet it had at last come home to him that all men might not be reasonable. He had tried reasoning but it might not work. There was only a slim chance.

They had taken his guns but they made no move to tie him up. At the first move to escape they'd empty their guns into him, and he knew it.

A half mile away, in thick brush near the mules, Susanna saw the sky turning gray. There had been no shooting, but Duncan had not joined them. If he could have come, he would have. He was hurt or a prisoner. Yet why would they want him a prisoner? It might be they would hold him to bring her back.

Tom awakened and looked nervously about, then saw her. "Ma! Where's Pa?"

"He did not come. I am afraid he is hurt or they have taken him."

"I could look. I could go back there. Nobody'd see me."

"We'll both go."

"No, Ma, you mustn't. You're bigger than me, and your skirts rustle. They'd never see me, or hear me."

"Wait . . . just a little longer."

Duncan would be with them if he could be with them. She was sure of that.

Nor did she dare leave this spot. Duncan had told them to come here, so if he arrived and there was no one he would start looking again. This was their base, here she was, here Duncan would come, and if Tom went he would come back to this place. And the mules and horses were here.

"All right, Tom," she said suddenly. "Go back to where we were last night. If you don't find your father, come right back here, for he expects us to be here."

After all, it should take Tom no more than thirty minutes, or perhaps an hour. He left quickly and faded into the brush. His very silence reassured her. After the first movement of the brush there was no further sound.

She was alone. More than a thousand miles from friends, relatives, all that was familiar. She was sitting alone in the forest, knowing only that her husband might be injured or dead and that she had let her son go off into the night, and that he might be killed.

She had the shotgun. She looked at the charges, still in place . . . unfired.

She snapped the gun together again and waited. She forced herself to be strong, forced herself to be calm. Panic, someone had once said . . . had it been Vallian? . . . only enters an empty mind, and panic was what she must fear now—only panic. She steeled herself for what might lie ahead, and slowly the loneliness and fear left her. Although she was still alone, she was prepared for what might come.

Coolly, she studied the possibilities. Duncan was dead? If so, she must avoid Shabbitt's men and get to Cherry Creek.

If he was a prisoner, she must contrive some way to free him.

If wounded, she must find him, hide him, and treat his wounds. During this period they must move as little as possible, remain hidden, and avoid leaving any tracks even if it meant hunger.

She must trust Tom. He was young, but he was strong for his years and had grown stronger with the hard work on the trip thus far. He had learned a great deal from Con Vallian, and from Duncan. He was good at slipping around in the woods and he might be the one to locate Duncan.

She got to her feet and moved away from the spot where she had been to a slightly higher place on the side of the mountain where she could watch the place where she and Tom had been. From where she now sat she could also see the approach to the hidden corral, although the horses and mules were not visible.

Slowly, the minutes went by. She kept alert, but at the same time began to speculate on how she could treat and feed a wounded man without showing herself.

Her thoughts returned to Tom. He was so young, so very young! Had she been foolish to let him go? He was her baby! Why, it was only . . . only a few years ago that she had rocked him to sleep in her arms, and now he had gone off in the woods searching for his father . . . alone.

Tom McKaskel was scared. He admitted it. He was also delighted, although he would not have told his mother so. He was looking for his father, but creeping through the woods was like playing Indian, only this was not play.

Tom was careful not to step on a branch that might break, a stone that might roll. He stayed low, as he moved from hiding place to hiding place. He was sure he was doing it well. He had covered more than a quarter of a mile and was sure he had not been seen.

He was wrong.

For the past fifty yards he had been watched by the Huron.

Searching for Vallian, whom he knew was somewhere near, the Huron saw the boy. At first he believed he might be going to Vallian, but then he realized the boy was searching for his father.

Standing close between two trees, his body merging with their darkness, he watched the boy moving from tree to tree. For a moment he hesitated, then turned deliberately away, leaving the boy to go his way.

After a moment, Huron turned in the direction from which the boy had come.

As the sky grew gray with approaching daylight, Red Hyle got to his feet. He felt surly and mean. He had waited too long, had wasted his time with this bunch of fools. He glanced at Doc Shabbitt, ugly distaste showing in his eyes, from across the fire Purdy seemed to be dozing, yet Red was not so sure. Purdy Mantle missed very little, and Red was sure that Purdy waited only for the opportunity to kill him.

Hyle suddenly turned and strode to his horse. Shabbitt made a move to rise and Hyle turned his head to look back over his shoulder. "Stay where you are! I got business to attend to!"

Duncan McKaskel started almost involuntarily to rise, but Ike was watching him like a cat. He would not make two feet before he'd be dead, and dead he would be of no use to Susanna or Tom.

"Where's he going?" he asked.

Ike grinned. It was an ugly, taunting grin. "After your woman. If'n she is with Vallian, he's as good as dead. If she ain't, he'll have her all to himself."

Protest would do no good. He sat back, trying to seem indifferent. Yet mentally he was searching every corner of camp, reaching out for any clue, any item that might help him to get away.

There was nothing.

Red Hyle swung into the saddle and turned his horse toward the trail. Within a moment he had found Duncan's trail and started off.

"Where's the Huron?" Purdy asked suddenly.

Doc shrugged. "Who knows? He just leaves . . . goes where he pleases, when he pleases." Doc let the minute pass and then said, carefully, "Red's no hand for sharin', is he?"

Ike threw a taunting glance at Doc. "Hate him, don't you? Why don't you shoot him then?"

Doc spat. "Him? He'll get hisself shot. Besides, we need him. He's mighty good with a gun."

"So's Purdy," Ike said. "I think maybe Purdy is better."

"He's not my meat," Purdy said quietly. "Get somebody else to do your killin'."

Duncan sat thinking of a way to escape when he looked up and saw Tom. He was in the trees, well back from the small clearing, and he was watching them.

Fear turned Duncan cold. If they got the boy, if they even saw him—

Chapter XIX

Con Vallian awakened in the clear, cold hour before daybreak. He lay still, listening. His horse was standing quietly, so he got up, brushed off the grass and leaves, then stretched and stretched again.

He took out his six-shooter and spun the cylinder. It was in fine shape. He loaded the empty chamber, making it six rounds. Then he took up his Winchester and wiped the dampness from it.

He stripped the saddle from the mustang and let the horse roll, then rubbed it down with a handful of dried grass, and saddled up again.

He had a bad, irritable feeling this morning. It might be the uncomfortable place in which he had slept, and it might be a premonition. Maybe everybody had pulled out during the night and all were gone. He put a foot into the stirrup and held it there.

He heard a horse trot by, not far off. Taking his foot down he turned swiftly. Red Hyle was just disappearing into the trees, seemingly following a trail.

Red Hyle . . . alone.

For several minutes he remained as he was, considering what that meant. If Red continued on that trail he would be very near to the mule corral.

Mounting, Con turned his horse and walked it along the edge of the trees, staying in the background so that he would not be easily seen.

He knew all about Red Hyle. He was a brute, and if he possessed any human feelings at all they had not made themselves obvious. His attitude was one of contempt for everyone but his sheer physical power and harsh manner allowed no room for opposition. Just nobody wanted any part of Red Hyle.

Vallian had been shooting since childhood and was a dead shot with any kind of a weapon. He was also gifted with dexterity, that natural coordination of hand and eye that permits a man to have exceptional skill with a gun. He never thought of himself as a gunfighter, never considered the use of guns as a goal to be attained. They were simply a part of his way of life and that of every man of his time.

He did pride himself on his skill as a tracker and a woodsman. He had believed he was second to none, and yet the Huron had twice come upon him without being detected. The thought rankled and worried him.

He drew up again, half under the shade of a cottonwood, his body and that of his horse dappled with sunshine and shadow. From even a few yards away he would be invisible.

It was then he saw the riders.

Doc Shabbitt was in the lead, behind him Ike and Purdy Mantle, and tied to a horse . . . Duncan McKaskel.

It was Duncan himself who started them after Hyle. Held a prisoner he could do no good, and if they stayed around they might discover Tom.

"What does he do now?" McKaskel asked curiously. "Do you sit waiting until he comes back? I thought you were all in this together."

Nobody said anything, but Doc shifted uncomfortably. "There's nothing in my wagon," he said, "nor with my wife, but if there was, he'd get it all."

"Shut your trap!" Purdy said irritably, then he looked over at Doc. "Well, we did all come out together. We all should see it through together."

"You mean, ride after Hyle? I don't think he wants comp'ny."

"To hell with him. We're all in this together."

"What if he gets sore? He said we should stay put."

"You takin' orders from him, Doc? I thought you was the leader. I say we all ride over there. I say we take McKaskel here. We started out together, and we'll finish the job together."

Ike and Purdy jerked McKaskel to his feet, thrust his hands behind him and tied them, then helped him on a horse. Leaving the horse standing, they all began saddling up. The area was so small that there was no chance of making a move even though McKaskel's horse was standing close under the trees.

Doc was in the saddle when Duncan McKaskel felt something tug on the rawhide bonds that held him, and then felt the sawing of a knife.

Tom's jack-knife. For weeks he had been planning on sharpening it for the boy but neglected it.

The boy sawed, then shifted position and began sawing on another strand without completing the first. McKaskel was cold with fear. If they caught the boy, they'd kill him, and he dared not even whisper. The boy was in the brush close against his horse's side, and presumably out of sight, yet a move of the horse might reveal him.

Suddenly Purdy turned his horse toward him. "All right, Mac, we'll go call on your wife. And Red Hyle."

They rode out, and he dared not look back. Gently, he tested the rawhide. The ropes held tight, yet he was sure they had been cut almost through, and a sudden jerk might part them. For a wild moment he considered it, then decided against it. He would be killed without helping anybody. He must wait until he could act to some purpose.

Con Vallian saw them ride past but was struck by only one factor. The Huron was not among them. The Huron must be somewhere in the woods and that meant he might be very close.

Hesitating, studying the woods with care, he saw nothing. He listened, he turned in the saddle and studied the wall of trees behind him . . . nothing. There was no doubt in his mind that the next time he saw the Huron one of them would die.

Over there! Something moved! Con slid his rifle from the scabbard and lifted it in his hands, waiting. Something was over there in the brush, something that could only be a man. He was ready to shoot, but he was not the sort to blast away at any chance movement. He wanted to see what he was shooting. He held the rifle ready, and waited.

Suddenly a small figure darted from the brush and ran across a portion of the clearing. It was Tom!

Con walked his horse from the brush toward the boy, keeping his eyes and ears alert for the Huron. Tom saw him coming, and pulled up.

"Tom, where's your mother?"

"Yonder. Over where they are going. Pa's tied, but I was cutting on the rawhide. With a good jerk he can break loose."

"Good. Let's ride over there."

He grasped the boy's hand and swung him to the saddle behind him, and then started on a fast lope for the corrals. Con rode with his rifle in his hands, for the Huron had to be close.

Turning into the trees, he dismounted. Tom slid to the ground. "You stay here, Tom. Stay with my horse."

"Aw!" Tom grabbed Vallian's arm. "Ma's over there! I've got to help!"

"You stay out of it!" Vallian said sharply. "There's going to be shooting, and there's no fun in it."

He touched his gun-butt, wetting his lips. He could hear the distant sound of voices, and taking his rifle in his hand, he started to walk closer.

Shabbitt had only now found the place, and Red Hyle was obviously angered.

Waiting back in the trees, well-hidden, Vallian listened, taking in the scene.

Susanna McKaskel had her back to a tree, and in her hands was a shotgun. Her face was white and strained, her eyes bright, but the gun was ready.

"Figured you might need he'p," Doc was saying. "After all, we started this here together, we figure to finish it the same way."

"You see it that way, too, Purdy?" Hyle was standing wide-legged, his hands on his hips. They were thick, powerful hands with red hair on the backs. His blunt, brutal features seemed to thrust forward.

"We're in it together, Red. If they've got anything, we want our share."

McKaskel was close to Shabbitt, and even as Con glanced that way he saw McKaskel's horse step over a little closer. If McKaskel's hands were still tied there was not much he could do, but if he could break loose he'd be in a fair position to jump Doc.

Con's eyes swept the scene again. Purdy, Ike, and Red Hyle. It was too tough a job even if McKaskel got Doc out of it.

Susanna had the shotgun, of course, and she might account for one. She had been quick enough to act when she swung that club on Booster.

"We've got your husband," Hyle said, turning to Susanna. "You put down that shotgun or I'll have Doc start cuttin' fingers off. Every time I count, he'll lose another finger. Now you goin' to drop it or not?"

Susanna's shotgun was steady. "Mister," she spoke quietly, "if you say *one*, you will never say *two*. By the time you open your mouth I will have blown you apart with both barrels of this shotgun. You know, Mr. Hyle, or whatever your name is, you make a big, wide target, and I don't think I like you, Mr. Hyle."

All the time Vallian kept thinking, *where is the Huron?* He looked all around him, but he could see nothing out of the ordinary.

It looked like a stalemate, but Con Vallian did not believe in stalemates. He held back, waiting. If the Huron moved in, then he would do likewise, otherwise he preferred to be the joker in the deck.

"Now," Susanna was cool, "you just back up and ride away, and when you go, leave my husband right where he is."

Nobody moved. There were four armed men and she was alone. How long before her nerve broke? How long before her arms tired and she lowered the shotgun?

She had obviously expected them to go, and when she spoke again, her voice was higher. "Go," she said, "or I'll shoot!"

Doc Shabbitt was smiling. It was a situation he liked, Con could see that, and especially as the shotgun was not pointed at him. "Ma'am," he said, "you better put that gun down. If you was to kill Red here, there'd still be the three of us.

"First off, I'd kill your husband. Then we'd just have things as we want them. If'n I was you, I'd just put down that there shotgun and hope we'll be easy on you."

What she would have done, Con Vallian never knew, for at that instant, Tom rushed up. "Ma! Give me that gun, I'll—!"

Her eyes went to Tom, and Red Hyle lunged for her. Duncan, bursting the sawed-through rawhide, spurred his horse to jump against Shabbitt, whose horse side-stepped into those of the Mantles. Duncan threw both arms around Doc and they went from the saddle to the ground.

Con Vallian snapped a quick shot at Hyle, missed, and swung the gun on Ike Mantle. Ike saw the rifle swinging to cover him and went down, Indian-fashion, on the far side of the horse, leaping it for the brush as he snapped a quick shot.

Hyle grabbed for the shotgun as Con swung his rifle for another shot, but Susanna clung to the gun. Red swung her violently, the shotgun tearing from her hands as she went into the brush. Con fired and the bullet burned across the back of Hyle's hand as the big gunman dove for the brush, grabbing for his six-shooter.

Susanna scrambled for the fallen shotgun as Shabbitt shook off her husband, and scrambled to his feet. He turned and grabbed at his horse, and Susanna shot at Hyle, then at Shabbitt.

Doc went sprawling, tried to get up, then sagged out on the grass, turning red beneath him.

Only Purdy remained, sitting his horse and offering to make no move.

Con Vallian strode down from the brush. "Ride out!" he shouted. "Ride out or make your fight!"

"I'll make my fight when I'm ready," Purdy said. "This here wasn't my idea."

He turned his horse and walked him from the camp.

Susanna was fumbling to get the empty cartridge casings from the shotgun. Tom stared, awed and frightened.

Slowly, Duncan got up and brushed himself off. "There wasn't much I could do. Arms numb," he said, "I just jumped my horse."

"Good thinking," Con said dryly, "that just about saved us all. Threw 'em all off stride."

Susanna stared in horror at Shabbitt. "Is he dead? I mean, did I—?"

Con walked over and turned Doc onto his back. The man was not dead, but soon would be. He had taken the shotgun blast through the lower part of the chest and part of the stomach.

Con Vallian turned around to meet Susanna's eyes. "Yes, ma'am, you did. And a good job it was, too."

"Let's get out of here," McKaskel said.

Chapter XX

On the seventh day following the difficulty in the woods, Duncan McKaskel had completed plowing an acre near the cabin for a vegetable garden and was planning a cornfield across the river on the flat near the old corral.

Con Vallian had been showing Tom how to cut long wedges to fit into cracks in the old cabin, and Susanna had taken time from other duties to bake a cake. Earlier, Tom had caught a half dozen trout from the stream, and the sun was bright over the cabin on the creek.

It was very quiet. Nobody had felt much like talking, but they all knew that Con had gone back and buried Doc Shabbitt where he had fallen, and that he had spent several days trying to pick up the trail of the vanished Red Hyle.

A dozen miles to the north not far from the Cherry Creek to Fort Laramie Trail, Purdy Mantle was seated by the fire waiting for Ike to return. Ike had ridden out after a deer or any meat that could be found, and to tell the truth, Purdy was glad to be alone.

He had been doing some thinking since the brief shoot-out and what he saw of himself did not appeal. He was good with a gun and he came from an outlaw clan, but outlawing had grown increasingly distasteful. He had said as much to Ike.

"It's no life for a man. On the dodge all the time."

"What you figurin' on?" Ike demanded. "You goin' to *work?*"

"What we do's often harder. I figure I'd like it. I ain't cut out for this."

Ike snorted, but said no more. Purdy was going soft he figured, and said as much, but Purdy merely shrugged.

He heard horses and straightened up. It was Ike, but he had Red Hyle with him.

Red had an angry-looking scratch along his cheekbone, and he rode kind of one-sided in the saddle. "Howdy," Purdy said, "looks like you caught a couple."

Hyle's expression was surly. "I didn't see you makin' no show of yourself, an' you're supposed to be good with a gun."

Purdy shrugged. "I never picked on women."

Hyle's face reddened. "What's that mean?"

"Nothin' at all," Purdy said quietly, "except I had no fuss with that woman. I didn't want her, an' you did. I didn't figure they had anything worth takin', an' I never did after maybe the first few days. It wasn't my idea to come along with them, and I was of no mind to get myself killed over it."

"If I thought you were pointin' that at me—!"

Ike interrupted. "That feller lied to us. He said his wife had taken off with Con Vallian."

"He prob'ly thought she had," Purdy said mildly. "He's been around here enough."

"Where was the Huron?" Ike grumbled. "He should have been there. I thought sure he'd come in there a-shootin'."

"I'm not through," Red Hyle said. "I'll bide my time."

"Leave them alone," Purdy advised. "They're trouble an' grief."

The smoke lifted straight toward the sky, and even the aspen leaves were still.

Purdy Mantle poked a stick in the fire. Here it was, right here, right now. He had seen it coming, and now Hyle was full of bitter anger and the need to explode. But then, if it had not been now it would have been something else later. He had known that all along.

"I've been shot at," he said mildly, his glance quizzical, almost amused. "I've been shot at, an' I've shot back."

Red Hyle straightened up, hands on his hips. "Have you now? You didn't do any shootin' back there in the woods. Was you scared?"

Purdy knew it was not to be avoided, and somehow deep inside, he wanted it. Just as much as Hyle did, he suspected. "No, I wasn't scared. I was too busy watchin' you run from that woman. She not only stood you off, Red Hyle, wanting none of you, but she made you run like a rabbit."

Hyle was on his feet and had the advantage, yet the moment his hand moved, Purdy knew. He had been poised and ready and he came up fast, and he drew fast—too fast. He had gotten his gun out swifter than had Hyle, but his first bullet went off as the gun was coming up and scattered fire. He never fired his second.

Hyle had palmed his gun coolly, swiftly, and when he shot it was unerringly, with just that split second of hesitation that made it matter. The first bullet took Purdy through the heart, the second an inch lower.

Red Hyle held his gun and glanced at Ike, who was roasting meat at the fire. "Funny thing," Ike said, "about Purd an' me. We was blood brothers, but we surely hadn't anything in common. We never really fancied each other."

Hyle slowly lifted the gun and dropped it back into its holster.

"Be different without him," Ike said. "We always sort of run together."

"He didn't want to go back, anyway," Red said, "an' I intend to go back. They ain't shut of me yet. That woman . . . I'll break all her fingers first. She'll learn not to throw down on me with no shotgun."

He stuck a piece of meat on a skewer. "You want to go back, Ike?"

"I was countin' on it," Ike said. "I never figured it no other way."

On the morning of the eighth day Tom collected wood. There was enough wood down so that no cutting was needed, so he went out into the edge of the timber and just picked up around where trees had fallen.

Duncan McKaskel crossed the stream with his plow and went to work on the cornfield he'd planned. It was easier plowing than expected, for there were few roots there in the bottom, and once he was through the sod the blade could cut deep into the good black earth. Duncan McKaskel wore a six-shooter and he had fastened a rifle scabbard on his plow handle.

Duncan looked down the dark earth of the furrows and was pleased. This was good land, fine land. He could get in a crop, and if he could keep the varmints away he would reap a good harvest. There was plenty of game, and there were fish in the river. Later in the year there would be wild strawberries and raspberries.

What he needed most were some cattle. There was enough grazing for a good-sized herd, and there was plenty of water. He had seen no cattle, and Con told him there was a meat shortage in Cherry Creek.

He started again and by noon he had plowed a fair chunk of land. He unhitched, left the plow where it was, and started back to the cabin for dinner.

Con was squatted on his heels beside the door as

Duncan came into the yard. "You take it pretty easy," McKaskel said, irritable from his own hard work.

Con smiled. "I've got no woman to support, and there's lots of country yonder that I ain't seen."

" 'A rolling stone gathers no moss,' " McKaskel quoted.

"Seems to me most of the moss grows on dead wood," Con said, grinning. "An' there's another quote, 'a wandering bee gets the honey.' "

Con pushed his hat back on his head. "Anyway, the food's good and it's a far piece to the next place where I could put my feet under a table."

"You've been very helpful," McKaskel said. "I don't know what we'd have done without you, but you must have some business, some place you want to go."

"Go? Oh, I got a thousand places to go! On'y I figure to set about for awhile, get some of the wrinkles out of my belly. Your wife surely does cook up a fine mess of vittles."

McKaskel had been stripping the harness from the mules as he talked. Now he carried it into the house and hung it on nails on the wall.

There was a tin wash-basin at the door. He poured water into it, rolled up his sleeves and began washing the dirt from his hands. His irritation remained with him, yet he knew it was in a large measure unjust. He was simply tired by the fact that he had put in a hard morning behind a plow and Con seemed to be merely sitting about.

Oh, he had cut some wood, and had brought in meat from time to time, but still—

"McKaskel," Con Vallian spoke suddenly and a little lower in tone, "you keep that rifle handy."

Something in his tone brought McKaskel up short. He looked down at the man who squatted beside him and said, "Have you seen something?"

"Tracks . . . only one or two. Fresh tracks. There's been somebody around."

"The Huron?"

"Could be. You keep that gun handy. That's a

mighty mean outfit and I never did feel they were
gone for good."

Duncan flipped water from his hands, then reached
for the towel. His hands had become very brown from
constant exposure, but his forearms, covered by sleeves
while working, were white as a woman's. He dried
them carefully, thinking.

"Is that why you're staying around?"

Vallian grinned. "I told you the food was good. Besides, you got a mighty handsome woman, there."

"I think Susanna is a very attractive woman," Duncan said quietly, "and she's my wife."

"That does make a difference," Vallian got up, with
a sigh. Filling the basin with fresh water, he washed
his own hands.

There was a small broken piece of mirror fastened
to the wall near the door and above the basin. As
he dried his hands he scanned the edge of the aspen
behind him. Being careful of a situation was as natural to him as eating.

Had he seen something move back there? Or was
it his imagination?

The leather thong was over the hammer of his gun,
and while drying his hands he slipped it off. Then
he hung up the towel, and taking the basin in his
left hand, tossed the water on the grass a few yards
away.

He flipped the basin one more time to get rid of the
last drops and then walked back to the cabin. He put
the basin down carefully, looking into the mirror as
he did so, and the glance caught Ike Mantle dodg-
ing from one tree to another, moving closer.

A surprise at meal-time, Ike behind him and the
others—?

Ike stepped from behind a tree, his rifle out in
front of him, coming up to firing position.

Con turned swiftly, drawing as he turned, and his
first bullet caught Ike Mantle just above the belt buck-
le. Ike started to fall, and the second bullet went in

under his right eye, and he was dead before he hit the ground.

Vallian turned swiftly at the slight sound beyond the corner of the cabin.

Red Hyle was there, a gun still in its holster, taken by surprise when their own surprise failed. He stopped dead in his tracks with Con Vallian's gun on him.

"Well, now. You got the drop. Why don't you shoot?"

"Just wanted to look at you, Red. I've just never seen you close up. They say you're a bad man with a gun, Red, but all I see is a murderin' skunk who chases after women and farmers."

"You can say that. You're holding the gun."

"Want a break, Red? Want an even break?"

"No!" It was Susanna's voice. "No, Con! Please!"

"Fat chance!" Red scoffed. "You'd never take a chance with Red Hyle! Why,—!"

With a flip of his hand, Con Vallian dropped the gun into its holster, and at the same moment yelled, *"Now, Red!"* And with a hand that scarcely stopped moving, he drew again and fired.

Red Hyle, caught by the unexpected action, lost a split second in realization. His hand, poised to reach, dropped for the gun-butt and started to lift when the bullet smashed him in the chest.

The big man scarcely staggered. His ugly smile parted his lips. "I got you! Dammit to hell, Vallian! *I got you!"*

The big gun came clear and was lifting as the second bullet smashed his arm, and a third hit him in the leg as he dropped to one knee to recover his lost gun.

"I got you, Vallian! Nobody ever beat Red Hyle!"

He straightened his legs and stood tottering, blood soaking the front of his shirt, dribbling down his sleeve.

He had his gun in his left hand and he swung it up

still smiling when Vallian's fourth and last shot hit him.

The big man staggered like a huge tree starting to fall, but he kept the grip on his gun.

Suddenly Tom leaped from the door behind Vallian. "Con! *Here!*"

The boy tossed him a six-shooter and Con caught it deftly. Red's gun bellowed, going off into the dirt at Con's boot-toe, and Con opened fire with the second gun. Bullet after bullet smashed into Hyle. He wavered, staggered, started to fall, but lifted the gun and through a mask of blood, aimed it at Vallian.

"Nobody ever . . . ever . . ." His voice trailed away and he swayed, slowly his knees buckled and he went to his knees on the ground and slowly straightened one leg and was dead.

"Vallian?" McKaskel came from the house. "Are you all right?"

Tom sat on the ground where he had fallen after throwing the gun to Vallian, staring at him, shocked.

Susanna stood in the door, her apron caught up in her hands, staring at him.

Thrusting McKaskel's pistol into his belt, Con began automatically thumbing shells into his own gun. Then he spun the cylinder and dropped it into its holster.

"Con? Look!" Susanna's voice was weak.

He turned sharply.

The Huron was riding up through the clearing, walking his horse. Across the saddle before him was a quarter of antelope. He walked his horse slowly forward, and when close by, turned his mount and handed the meat to an astonished Duncan.

"It has been a pleasure," he said quietly, and turning his horse rode away down the clearing toward the river.

ABOUT THE AUTHOR

LOUIS L'AMOUR, born Louis Dearborn L'Amour, is of French-Irish descent. Although Mr. L'Amour claims his writing began as a "spur-of-the-moment thing," prompted by friends who relished his verbal tales of the West, he comes by his talent honestly. A frontiersman by heritage (his grandfather was scalped by the Sioux), and a universal man by experience, Louis L'Amour lives the life of his fictional hero. Since leaving his native Jamestown, North Dakota, at the age of fifteen, he's been a longshoreman, lumberjack, elephant handler, hay shocker, flume builder, fruit picker, and an officer on tank destroyers during World War II. And he's written four hundred short stories and over eighty books (including a volume of poetry).

Mr. L'Amour has lectured widely, traveled the West thoroughly, studied archaeology, compiled biographies of over one thousand Western gunfighters, and read prodigiously (his library holds more than two thousand volumes). And he's watched thirty-one of his westerns as movies. He's circled the world on a freighter, mined in the West, sailed a dhow on the Red Sea, been shipwrecked in the West Indies, and has been stranded in the Mojave Desert. He's won fifty-one of fifty-nine fights as a professional boxer and pinch-hit for Dorothy Kilgallen when she was on vacation from her column. Since 1816, thirty-three members of his family have been writers. And, he says, "I could sit in the middle of Sunset Boulevard and write with my typewriter on my knees, temperamental I am not."

Mr. L'Amour is re-creating an 1865 Western town, christened Shalaka, where the borders of Utah, Arizona, New Mexico, and Colorado meet. Historically authentic from whistle to well, when it is constructed, it will be a live, operating town, as well as a movie location and tourist attraction.

Mr. L'Amour now lives in Los Angeles with his wife Kathy and their two children, Beau and Angelique.